SPECIAL MESSAGE TO READERS

THE ULVERSCROFT FOUNDATION
(registered UK charity number 264873)

was established in 1972 to provide funds for research, diagnosis and treatment of eye diseases. Examples of major projects funded by the Ulverscroft Foundation are:-

- The Children's Eye Unit at Moorfields Eye Hospital, London
- The Ulverscroft Children's Eye Unit at Great Ormond Street Hospital for Sick Children
- Funding research into eye diseases and treatment at the Department of Ophthalmology, University of Leicester
- The Ulverscroft Vision Research Group, Institute of Child Health
- Twin operating theatres at the Western Ophthalmic Hospital, London
- The Chair of Ophthalmology at the Royal Australian College of Ophthalmologists

You can help further the work of the Foundation by making a donation or leaving a legacy. Every contribution is gratefully received. If you would like to help support the Foundation or require further information, please contact:

THE ULVERSCROFT FOUNDATION
The Green, Bradgate Road, Anstey
Leicester LE7 7FU, England
Tel: (0116) 236 4325

website: www.foundation.ulverscroft.com

FOLLOW YOUR DREAM

Steph has a successful career, a smart London flat and a good social life. After being badly hurt by the man she loved, she is determined never to let it happen again. When she inherits her Aunt Rose's old cottage in the village where she grew up, she decides to take two weeks to put everything in order and sell up — but then she meets the attractive Rick Jameson . . . Steph has some difficult decisions to make, and things are not necessarily what they seem.

JEAN ROBINSON

FOLLOW YOUR DREAM

Complete and Unabridged

LINFORD
Leicester

First published in Great Britain

First Linford Edition
published 2013

*A catalogue record for this book is available
from the British Library.*

ISBN 978–1–4448–1686–0

Published by
F. A. Thorpe (Publishing)
Anstey, Leicestershire

Set by Words & Graphics Ltd.
Anstey, Leicestershire
Printed and bound in Great Britain by
T. J. International Ltd., Padstow, Cornwall

This book is printed on acid-free paper

A Two-Week Stay

On her last visit to Aunt Rose's cottage, Simon had been with her. The memory still stung. Steph had to wipe that memory out for good, so she turned her thoughts to her aunt.

'We all kept an eye on her,' Elsie had told her after the funeral. 'She was a lovely lady and so independent. She wouldn't ask for help, so we did what we could.'

Just like me, Steph thought; fiercely independent, loath ever to accept the fact that she needed anything from anyone. Simon had told her this when he left.

'You don't need me, Steph,' he'd said. 'You don't need anyone.' The woman he'd left her for was a pretty blonde who hung on his every word. Well, she couldn't be like that if she tried, so the relationship wouldn't have worked. But it had broken her heart when they'd parted.

She had been so deep in thought that it seemed the car had driven itself through the outskirts of the town and down the winding road that led to Marshland village and then out towards the sea. Green Lane was pitted, and she tried to avoid the worst of the puddles left by the recent downpour, but now sunshine was breaking through the clouds and giving a bright sparkle to the hedgerows where she had picked wild flowers as a child.

There was a stony patch at the side of the cottage where she crunched her car to a halt. She felt some apprehension as to what she would find inside. Steph remembered visits with her mum. She'd played in the big wild garden — a wonderful place for hide and seek. Aunt Rose always found her, but never without a lot of hunting. There'd been home-made scones for tea and, on winter afternoons, a huge fire burning in the grate. The visits became less frequent as she reached her teens.

Then, after moving to London to work, they had stopped altogether. This was going to be painful, she knew, but it had to be done.

Stretching her limbs and taking in some breaths of sea air, Steph viewed Bramble Cottage in the sunshine; white pebble-dash walls, grey slate roof, doors and windows with peeling paint. The whole thing was encased in hedges six feet high and in desperate need of cutting.

The gate was hanging off its hinge and she had to lift it to get past. Somebody must have tried to close it and it had stuck. The small front garden behind the hedge was just a patch of overgrown grass and straggling rose bushes, not the way Steph remembered it. Rose had loved her garden and taken pride in keeping it well tended.

Something stopped Steph from immediately opening the front door and going in. The sun was setting on a lovely June day and its low rays caught the white-washed walls just above the window and cast a pretty rosy glow. Then she noticed blossom just peeping round the side. Not being a gardener, she had no idea what it was, but it lifted her spirits and she sniffed it and held some in her hands.

It was a difficult scramble to get past the rubbish that had accumulated between the side hedge and the cottage wall, but when she got round the back she was devastated to see the wilderness of shrubs, overgrown hedges, a dilapidated greenhouse and a patch of lawn just outside the back door that had grown round the wooden table and chairs that were abandoned there. She could see how it had got its name. The whole area was covered in brambles. Her heart sank when she thought of her poor aunt trying to cope with this and she dreaded what she would find inside.

The cottage smelled musty and closed up; there were dishes in the sink and the scrubbed wooden table was cluttered with an assortment of papers and various jars and tins. Poor Rose hadn't been coping very well, that was obvious. Elsie had told her how her aunt's eyesight had not been good and she had suffered from arthritis, which would account for the state of the place. When she tried to open the window over the sink she could see the frame was rotten.

The dining-room was bright and airy with a polished table in front of a big window overlooking the garden, whilst the front room, with its low beamed ceiling and brick fireplace, had only tiny latticed windows which let in very little light. This room was as she remembered it — an old saggy chair piled with cushions near the fireplace and an overstuffed sofa which was reserved for visitors. The curtains were faded, the carpets threadbare, the whole place having an air of neglect.

Flopping down on the chair and, pulling a shawl round her shoulders, she slumped into misery. The evening light slanting through the windows showed up the dusty old dresser, another threadbare easy chair stacked with cushions, and ornaments on every surface with envelopes and cards stuffed behind them in a mess of clutter. The pile of newspapers and magazines by the fire were yellowing at the edges and the rug in front of it had burn marks where sparks had landed. She groaned inwardly. She had to sort all this lot out.

There was a knock, the back door opened and a cheery voice shouted, 'Anyone at home?'

Steph smiled to herself. Elsie wouldn't wait to be asked in. She was used to just popping in uninvited.

'I brought you some hotpot. Don't suppose you'll want to cook tonight.' She was still the jolly lady Steph remembered, well into her 80s now, rather plump with a skirt that seemed to be stretched to the limit and ankles overlapping her very sensible shoes.

Steph took the dish wrapped in a tea towel and put it on the kitchen table. It smelled good and she was hungry.

'You staying a bit this time, are you?' Elsie asked, perching on one of the kitchen chairs.

'Yes, I have some holidays due so I thought I'd come and clean it up a bit.'

'Needs more than cleaning up, does this place.' Elsie shook her head. 'Now, you just let us know if you need ought. Our Jim'll come round. He's right handy is our Jim.'

Steph filled the kettle and placed it on the hob. She put a match to the gas and was amazed when it flared into life.

They had their tea sitting at the kitchen table, then Elsie stood up and looked round, taking in all that was needed.

'You've a job on yer hands and that's for sure. Now, is there ought else ye need tonight?'

'I'm fine, Elsie, really. I'll take it easy this evening and make a start tomorrow.'

When Elsie bustled out of the door Steph began to wash up and she couldn't help thinking about the past.

Her mum had been so different from her aunt. Nobody would ever have thought of them as sisters. Steph and her mum had lived in a nice bungalow in the village down a quiet lane; just the two of them after her dad had died. It was tiny, even smaller than the cottage, but her mum kept it immaculate, everything tasteful and in its place, the way Steph kept her flat. But Rose was too busy making jam, pickling onions and digging her vegetable patch to have time for dusting. But the sisters had been close.

She heated up the hotpot then climbed the stairs. It had been a long day. With some trepidation she opened the door to her aunt's bedroom. She closed it again quickly. She'd deal with that tomorrow. The other bedroom was more or less as she remembered it, with just a single bed and a set of drawers. Grateful that there was clean bedding on it, she undressed quickly and slithered between the sheets.

Just as she was drifting into an

exhausted sleep, Greg phoned to check she'd arrived safely. He was a kind man, but he was getting a bit too possessive. Her friend, Greta, said he was a good catch and that she ought to encourage him.

'He's crazy about you, anyone can see that, and he's loaded,' Greta had said. But Steph was adamant that it was platonic. She'd made that clear to Greg from the start.

They'd known each other for years and had drifted together after Simon had left and Greg had given her a lot of support. They both enjoyed going to the theatre and had many mutual friends, so it was a comfortable and convenient arrangement. The last thing Steph wanted was another disastrous romance. She enjoyed her freedom and her work and her Hampstead flat. At thirty-four she had it all worked out and she wasn't going to let anything or anyone get in the way.

When she woke, sun was pouring in at the window. It was eleven o'clock.

She never lay in bed this late. There were things to do. She jumped out of bed and headed for the shower until she remembered there wasn't one. The small bathroom contained only a toilet, wash basin and huge enamel bath, so a quick wash would have to do until she managed to coax the boiler into life.

The kitchen was streaming with light and there was a bundle wrapped up in a cloth on the table. She poked at it gingerly and it was warm. Warm rolls and a pot of home-made jam. Elsie had been in again.

Taking her tea and the rolls into the front room she tried to decide which was most uncomfortable, the over-stuffed sofa or the sagging chair, then decided to sit on the floor. Looking at the clutter on the mantelpiece it was hard to know where to start. It would take longer than two weeks to sort this place out. And then what was she to do with it? Sell it, she supposed. It wouldn't be easy to sell in this state, but if she cleaned it up a bit and cleared out the rubbish then she might be in with a chance.

On the other hand she might as well get hold of an estate agent as soon as possible, as it would take time to get it on the market and it would give her the incentive she needed to sort it out.

Throwing her plate into the sink, she grabbed her bag and went out to the car. No time like the present. Her boss was difficult about them taking time off at short notice and she didn't want to upset him just when her career was advancing. She'd worked too hard to get where she was.

She could hear her mum's voice in her head telling her, 'Whatever you choose to do in life, do it to the best of your ability.' Her dad had said that the best thing he could give her was a good education. She'd been sent to a private school in Southport and loved every day she was there.

On leaving with good A-levels, she'd joined Greystone Insurance in the claims department. Then, after taking all the financial exams she could, she had worked her way up to area manager with a salary big enough to rent an upmarket flat in Hampstead, run her car and have enough left over for foreign holidays and a good social life. The next step up the ladder would probably put her in a bracket where she could afford a mortgage on a house.

The girl in the estate agent's was friendly and said she'd send someone round the next day. Satisfied she had set things in motion, she decided to have a wander round the town before heading back.

It was a good feeling to be back in Southport. It all seemed different and yet the same. Lord Street was still impressive with its wide pavements, Victorian arcades and lovely shops.

The side streets leading up to the promenade were lined with shops selling ice-cream and she indulged herself in a huge cone. Then she was standing beside the Marine Lake and remembering when she'd rowed a boat on it as a child. It had been a good childhood here with her mum and aunt, but now they were both gone. She shook herself. This wasn't getting the cottage cleared.

In a surprisingly short time she had achieved quite a lot. It really wasn't dirty, just messy, and after she'd filled three bin liners it looked quite different. Elsie came to see if she needed any help, and before waiting for an answer had rolled up her sleeves and was on her hands and knees on the old tiled floor. Then she set to on clearing out the food cupboard and scrubbing the shelves.

'Now, you come round at six. I've a nice piece of beef cooking in the oven and there's plenty for three of us.'

Steph wondered if she should decline this invitation as Elsie had already done so much for her, but she was feeling tired and hungry and the thought of company for the evening was tempting, so she said she would be happy to join them.

That night she slept better than she could ever remember, even wrapped in old-fashioned blankets and on a lumpy mattress. It was another lovely day, and while the kettle boiled she thought of all the things she could do to make the cottage more comfortable, then decided it really wasn't worth it. Once she'd cleared the place out she would sell it and never come here again. All she needed to do was make it presentable and make sure there wasn't anything important hidden amidst all the stuff.

At ten o'clock there was a knock on the door. It was the estate agent. She couldn't complain about his time-keeping. If he was as efficient at selling the place then her worries would be over.

'Bradley Pyke, come to look at your cottage,' the young man said as he stepped into the tiny hall and offered his hand. 'Now, where shall we start?' He had to duck to get into the living-room and looked decidedly awkward perched on the edge of the sofa.

They went over the preliminaries and

he wrote down some details and quoted her various options regarding commission rates and advertising.

'Whatever it takes,' she said. 'I just want to get rid of it as quickly as possible.'

He raised an eyebrow.

'Really. I think it's rather wonderful. It's a bit run down, but you could make it into a very cosy home.'

For some reason this annoyed her.

'I have a home,' she snapped, then regretted her tone.

He shrugged and, after giving her a questioning look, returned to filling in his paperwork.

'OK, I'll measure up now,' he said. 'These beams are amazing,' he added, stroking them lovingly.

'Are they?' Steph found the low ceilings rather oppressive, and she imagined he would have found the need to duck all the time an irritation.

'I suppose you have a minimalist flat if you live in London,' he said dismissively.

She resented that.

'I have a very smart flat in Hampstead. And no, I do not have a lot of clutter. I prefer clean lines and calm decor.'

Again he raised an eyebrow and a hint of amusement played round his mouth, but he said nothing and continued to size the place up.

'Well, in its present state it won't sell easily. I'd suggest you clean it up a bit, sort the garden out and maybe give it a lick of paint. As to price, what were you hoping for?' Bradley asked.

'I want you to sell it as it stands. I don't have time to make any of the changes you suggest. As to price, I thought that was your department.'

He looked taken aback this time and she wasn't surprised. What had made her act so out of character? She wasn't usually rude to people.

'Well, if that's what you want. I don't think it would go for more than sixty thousand in its present condition.' His friendly manner had evaporated and he avoided looking at her.

She immediately regretted antagonising him, but felt at a loss as to how to remedy the situation.

'That's fine,' she said.

She saw him out and watched as his small car disappeared down the lane. Once the place was sold she could bank the money and forget about it. Sixty thousand wasn't to be sniffed at, even with her income.

Greg phoned again that evening wanting to know when she would be home.

'I told you I intend to stay for two weeks. I've a lot to do here,' was her reply.

'But you said you were just going to put the place on the market, sort out any personal stuff and then leave it to the estate agent. How long can that take?'

She could visualise him standing there holding the phone, a typical bank manager, middle-aged at forty.

'There's a lot more to do. I can't

leave it in this state. It's a mess. I'll be home in a couple of weeks, like I said.'

'I hope you haven't forgotten Greta's barbecue a week on Saturday.'

She hadn't forgotten. If she was home in time, she'd go. She'd explained this to Greta and she'd been fine about it. Greg was becoming too possessive for her liking and she'd have to clear that up with him.

'I'll be there,' she said to keep him happy and bring the call to an end.

She took a glass of wine out into the garden and perched on a bit of wall by the pond where she could enjoy the sun setting over the apple trees. She'd made good progress with the inside of the cottage with the help of Elsie, and she'd sorted out all the details the agency had asked of her. A surveyor was booked for tomorrow morning and Bradley had phoned to say he already had someone interested in the property and he was bringing them round on Wednesday afternoon for a sneak preview.

But would they be interested in it,

the state it was in? Maybe Bradley was right. She'd just have to see. She would continue to clean it up and sort it out until her two weeks were up. In fact, she was finding it strangely therapeutic, a complete change from the hectic life she lived in London.

Plonking herself down inside the cottage with a plate of salad, she switched on the TV, but she was so tired by nine that she made a cup of tea and went to bed with her book.

The Gardener

Tuesday morning was bright and sunny again and Steph felt much more optimistic. There might just be time to pop along to the village store for some much-needed groceries before the surveyor was due. She'd seen it on her way through the village; the corner shop she remembered from childhood with its bow window and green painted door.

A pleasant-looking woman with short dark hair and a healthy complexion was stacking a shelf with packets of biscuits and chatting to another older lady who stood watching, so Steph filled her basket and made her way to the counter. The lady looked at Steph then picked up her shopping bag and made for the door. 'Bye, then, Bel,' she said and left.

'The Lancashire's lovely and crumbly,' Bel offered as Steph looked inside the glass case at the selection of cheeses and cold meat.

Steph sighed.

'Ah, yes, I used to come here for some of that when I was ten. Mum used to send me.'

Bel raised an eyebrow.

'You come from these parts, then, do you? You don't sound local.'

'I've lived in London for the past twenty years.'

'Ah, that explains it. Work, I suppose. Not much going in these parts. You'll remember my mother, I expect.'

Steph racked her brain. The shop inside had looked quite different then, with an old-fashioned wooden counter and everything stacked on shelves behind it. The elderly lady had been very small and always wore an apron. What was her name? Mrs Ball, that was it.

'Yes, I do, now I come to think. She was always rushing about chatting to everyone. And she used to let me taste a bit of the cheese before she wrapped it up.'

Bel laughed.

'That was Mum.'

'Anyway, the cheese looks lovely and I'll have some ham, too. I don't want to have to cook while I'm here.'

Bel began to cut a chunk off the slab of cheese and wrap it for her.

'You putting it on the market? Don't suppose you want to live in it. Sad about your aunt. She was a lovely lady.'

Steph felt a stab of guilt. Why had she left it so long?

She paid for her shopping and thanked Bel. Outside in the sunshine she choked back the tears. All these memories and emotions. She needed to get stuck into some hard work and get it out of her system, so she set off at a brusque pace in the direction of home.

The surveyor didn't take long to complete his work and told her he'd make a full report which she would receive in a few days' time.

'Bit of dry rot in the beams. Needs treating fairly urgently. Needs rewiring, too. And the plumbing really isn't up to standard. Roof seems sound. Just a few slates loose. Not a big job.' He'd left with a smile and handshake.

Steph sank into the chair. He made it all sound so easy. But that entailed a massive amount of work and expense. Who would buy it once they'd seen his report? And how could she ever afford to have all that work done? It would certainly eat up the savings she'd put aside for the trip to Canada she and Greg had talked about for next year. What on earth was she going to do?

Elsie appearing at the kitchen door just at that moment was a welcome relief.

'You look a bit down, lass,' she said with a frown.

Steph told her about the survey.

'And the garden's beyond me. How do I clear away a broken-down greenhouse and sort that wilderness of brambles? What am I going to do, Elsie?'

Tears of frustration were coming and she tried in vain to hold them back. But when Elsie put an arm round her shoulder the flood gates opened. Elsie soothed her and let her sob it all out.

'I've inherited a headache,' she said between sobs.

As usual Elsie had an answer.

'Right, now! First of all, the garden. I'll send Rick along. He's good with gardens.'

An hour later a truck pulled up outside and a man jumped down from the cab and ambled up the path. He had a weathered look about his face and wore old jeans and a T-shirt. The sun glinted on his short curly hair and Steph watched through the window as he ambled up to the door. She wished she had made more effort instead of just dousing her face in cold water and tying her curls back in a pony tail.

'Rick, the gardener, at your service,' he said with a wide grin as she opened the door to him.

His handshake was firm and warm and his blue eyes held hers for a moment, giving her a very strange feeling. She quickly shook herself back to reality.

'Hello. Come in,' she mumbled as he eased past her through the front room into the kitchen.

She stood beside him as he looked out over the garden, weighing it up. He was a little taller than her, which made her feel good.

'Lot of work out there.' She sighed.

He looked down at her and smiled, his eyes kind, his mouth sensitive, the sort of man who had no idea how attractive he was.

'Not too bad. I could soon have it cleared,' he said.

'Could you?' Why was she sounding so pathetic instead of her usual business-like self.

'Would you like me to make a start tomorrow?'

'Yes, that would be great.' She hadn't even asked him for a quotation. Somehow it didn't seem appropriate. He seemed like the sort of man you could trust.

'I could even bring the trailer along

and we could make a start this afternoon if you like.'

She agreed. If it speeded things up
and got the job done cheaper then that
would be a good thing, wouldn't it?

Elsie called in on her way to the shop
and asked if she needed anything. They
stood out at the front and chatted for a
while and Steph told her about Rick's
visit.

'He's a good lad,' Elsie told her. 'Had
some bad luck recently, but he's getting
back on his feet now.'

Steph would have liked to have found
out more but decided it was best to
keep this to a business arrangement.

She changed into old jeans ready for
the gardening and plastered sun cream
on her arms and nose. This sunshine
was intense; great for enhancing the
highlights in her hair, but no good for
her fair skin. She peered in the cracked
mirror she'd found in Rose's bedroom
and reached for her make-up bag, then
grasped it firmly and stuffed it back in
the drawer.

Rick arrived with his truck and all the equipment needed to clear the garden. He gave her a pair of shears and told her to hack away at the brambles while he started clearing the greenhouse of broken glass.

Once she'd chopped down as much as she could of the tangle of weeds and could see the roots, she began to yank at them to try to get them out. He came up beside her and helped heave at the cluster of stems she had in her hand.

'No good,' he said. 'We have to dig at the roots now. These are too deep to pull out.'

He was so close she could feel the heat from his body, and when his bare arm touched hers she gave an involuntary shiver. He moved away to get the garden fork from the shed and came back to dig at the offending roots. She heaved as he dug and, when it gave way, she tumbled against him and they both laughed as he steadied her.

'Shall I get us a cold drink?' she offered.

He stretched his back and smiled at her.

'Sounds good.'

In the kitchen she took a few deep breaths. This was proving to be more enjoyable than she'd thought. She opened the bottle of shandy she'd bought at the shop that morning and arranged some biscuits on a plate.

The old garden table and a couple of the chairs seemed sound enough, so she brought out the tray and called to Rick. He was continuing to load the wheelbarrow but heard her and ambled over to where she was sitting and took a long slug of the shandy.

'My favourite,' he said, sinking on to the other chair.

It was lovely sitting there in the warm sunshine, overlooking the wilderness they were trying to tame.

'It's rather beautiful in its way, isn't it?' she said. 'That bit at the end is like a wild flower meadow.'

He smiled.

'We don't have to clear all of it. We

could leave some for the insects.'

'Would that be acceptable to a buyer?' she asked.

'You're not going to move into it yourself?' he asked.

'No, I have a flat in Hampstead and I work in the city.'

'Ah, one of the yuppie crowd,' he joked.

'I work for an insurance company as an account manager.' It sounded pretentious, but being classed as a yuppie had put her on the defensive.

'Sounds high powered. What do you actually do?'

'I deal with financial advisers and tell them about the type of investments my company offer, and then I support them when dealing with their clients. It's mostly pension schemes and investments.'

'Do you enjoy it?'

'I love it. It's a challenge and a big responsibility. You can't afford to get anything wrong when people are investing millions of pounds with you.'

'I can see you're a very clever girl. I expect you make a lot of money.' He got up and wandered back to his work.

Why had he reacted like that? What was wrong with enjoying your job and being prepared to take responsibility?

By six o'clock she was exhausted. The garden certainly looked a lot better and the greenhouse was ready for new glass. All the rubbish was in Rick's trailer trundling back down the lane. Steph decided it was time to test out the plumbing and fill the old cast-iron bath for a long soak.

Two hours later she was roused from a deep sleep by the phone ringing. When she eventually remembered where she was and where the phone was located, her voice sounded groggy as she mumbled a rather feeble hello.

It was Greta.

'How's it going, Steph?'

'Oh, OK, really. Sorry, I'd just nodded off.'

'At eight in the evening? Good heavens, Steph, country air must be having a strange effect on you.'

'It's sea air,' she reminded her. 'And I've been digging the garden all day. That's why I'm tired.'

There was a hoot of laughter on the other end of the line.

'Gardening? You are joking.'

'Well, I've just been doing a bit. Have to clear it up before I can put it on the market.'

'Can't you get a bloke to do it for you?'

'Actually I have. But he needs me to help him. I'm quite enjoying it. Good exercise. Beats going to the gym.'

'Oh, yeah!' Steph heard the amusement in her voice.

'Look, Greta, I might not make your barbecue. I'm sorry but I really do have a lot to do here and I need all the time I can spare. But we'll have a get together at mine as soon as I get back.'

They said their goodbyes and Steph put down the receiver. Greta was totally outrageous and a wonderful friend and she hoped she hadn't upset her. Well, at least she'd told her now and had warned Greg as well so she could relax here in the cottage for the whole two weeks and travel back ready for work on the Monday morning.

Still feeling tired, she made a cup of coffee and wandered up the stairs to bed. Rick was coming round first thing in the morning and she wanted to be rested and ready to start again. They were going to tackle the pond tomorrow and the grass outside the kitchen door.

When she tried to get out of bed the next morning she could hardly move. Slowly, as she dressed and made some tea, the stiffness eased a bit. The last thing she needed now was to be incapacitated when there was so much to do, and people coming round to view the place this afternoon.

Rick was there before she had finished her cup of tea.

'Come on,' he teased. 'We have work to do.'

She was growing to like his easy

manner and realised that they would soon turn the chaos into some sort of order. Even though he kept telling her what to do, it did seem they were working as a pair, and he sensed what she wanted without her having to spell it out.

They worked side by side, only breaking for a sandwich at lunch, and the area outside the cottage looked much nicer now the grass was cut. They'd uncovered some tubs full of plants that had been struggling to survive under the brambles, and Rick had re-potted them and put them by the table.

'They'll come on now they have some light,' he assured her.

'We need some colourful flowers to brighten them up,' she said.

'Geraniums would be good. You can get them in so many colours and they'll flower all summer.'

'And those hanging baskets could do with replacing. They must have looked lovely when Rose put them up, but now they're falling apart.'

'The Virginia creeper round the corner there needs a good trim. It'll look a treat in the autumn. And if I cut back the climbing rose it will produce more flowers.'

'It's such a pretty cottage, isn't it? I can see why Rose loved it so much. Fancy living in one place all your life. Rose was born here, looked after my gran until she died then stayed on. Hardly anyone does that these days.'

Rick was looking at her indulgently and smiling.

'You really are enjoying this, aren't you? And not a bad worker for a city girl,' he teased. She tried to look stern and ended up laughing. 'Come on, let's get going. We won't get anything done at this rate.'

She was covered in dust and cobwebs from clearing out the shed when the middle-aged couple arrived to view the house. They were neatly dressed and looked rather disapprovingly at the front garden and windows before they had even stepped inside the hall. Apologising for the state it was still in, Steph showed them round, but they made very little comment. When she opened the kitchen door for them to go into the garden, they hesitated.

'I don't think we need to see any more,' the plump little lady said without a smile. 'It really isn't what we are looking for, is it, Patrick?'

Steph saw them out and felt deflated. Well, what had she expected?

Rick was pulling handfuls of slime out of the pond and looked up as she came back out into the garden.

'No luck, then?' he asked.

She shrugged.

He wiped his hands on the grass and looked down at her in a way that made her feel he cared, that he shared her disappointment. They stood surveying their work in the warmth of the afternoon sun and her spirits began to lift.

'We've done well today, so why don't we knock off and go for a drink?' he suggested.

She needed a break and it seemed like a good idea.

'I wouldn't mind trying the local pub.'

But Rick had other ideas.

'Where are we going?' she asked as they sped round the winding lanes out of the village in his battered old car.

'Somewhere I think you'll like,' he told her with a sly smile on his face.

That smile made her feel young and carefree again. How long was it since she'd sat in a car with a man who was taking her out for a casual drink on a summer afternoon? She leaned back in the old leather seat and relaxed, not caring where he took her, content to be with him.

'There's a new bar on the promenade in Southport. I thought we'd try that,' he told her. 'The local pub's OK, but I go there every day.'

He found a parking space and held the door for her as she eased herself out, her back still stiff from all the exertion of the past few days, but it didn't feel as bad now. She must be getting used to the work. Then to her surprise he took her hand and led her along the promenade. It felt warm and good and when he smiled down at her it made her feel happy and secure.

'There's the old swimming baths I used to go to,' she told him and her mind was back again to those days of training when she had got up at six in the morning, cycled the seven miles to the swimming pool to train for the squad, then on to school, a further two miles out of town.

'You're a swimmer, then, are you?' he asked.

'Not any more.' She sighed.

'Why the sigh?'

'Oh, just thinking about how life has changed. More a quick session in the gym after work now if I'm lucky.'

He gave her hand a squeeze and looked at her.

'No family, then?'

'No, not in my plans at all. I love my job too much. Can't ever see how I could combine the two.'

'Most people manage it.'

She shrugged.

'I know. I just don't see it as me. I think I'm too selfish.' She didn't want to explain about the heartache she'd endured when Simon had left and how she would never take that risk again.

They walked in silence for a while, through the gardens which were just coming into bloom and keeping as close to the beach as they could. He still held on to her hand as they paused to look out over the endless miles of golden sands to the invisible sea and it felt good.

'I've cantered some miles along that beach,' she said.

'An equestrian, too?' he teased.

She laughed.

'No, not really. Just that my parents encouraged me to try everything with the idea that eventually I'd find the one I was good at.'

'And did you?'

'I suppose so. My job's stressful at

times and I get very tired, but I've definitely found what I'm good at and can't ever imagine doing anything else.'

As they stood there he let her hand go and put his arm round her shoulder. She leaned into him.

'What about you, then?' she asked.

He looked straight ahead of him out to sea and squeezed her shoulders slightly.

'Nothing much to tell. I live in the village, garden and do any other odd jobs people want doing. That's about it.'

She felt there was more, but wasn't going to probe. It was a lovely afternoon and she was happy to be here with him and just enjoy the moment. There was plenty in her past she wouldn't want to talk about, either. Elsie had said he'd had a bit of bad luck recently and he obviously didn't want to talk about it so she let it go.

The bar he took her to was overlooking the sea through large plate-glass windows.

'You told me how much you missed being beside the sea, so I thought you could have your fill of it here.'

Sitting at a small table looking out over the expanse of golden sand, she felt content. Seagulls perched on the railings round the terrace in front of them and there was a view of the pier running along the sand to meet the sea. Rose hadn't just given her a cottage, but had opened her eyes to a way of life she had forgotten existed. She had only known Rick for a couple of days and yet she felt comfortable with him.

They sat in companionable silence until the sun had dipped well beyond the horizon and the soft red glow was disappearing into dusk.

'Shall we make tracks and get back?' he asked.

She was tired and ready for home so readily agreed. He dropped her off at the cottage with a gentle kiss on the cheek, and as she waved him on his way she smiled to herself at the thought of tomorrow.

A Surprising Discovery

By 11 a.m. the next morning there was still no Rick and Steph felt disappointed. She'd made a special effort with her clothes and make-up and she had sandwiches in the fridge and had made a start on the tangle of brambles at the far end of the garden. Determined not to mind if he came or not, she struggled on alone and managed to clear quite a big patch by midday.

By this time she was cross. The least he could have done was to let her know he wasn't coming. She also felt hurt because she thought he cared for her, that they had a friendship which would make this two weeks working together pleasant. But she'd read the signals all wrong. With a feeling of self reproach for being so naive, she blinked back the tears and resolved to carry on and tackle the rest of the garden.

By three o'clock she stood back and surveyed her work. Not bad for a city girl. Wiping a dirty hand across her face and throwing the saw on the ground, she went into the kitchen to get a drink from the fridge. She was so tired she couldn't do anymore today. Tomorrow she would probably not even be able to get out of bed, but she was satisfied with what she had done. Yet she still worried about why Rick hadn't come.

Just then there was a creaking sound of the gate and he appeared round the corner of the cottage just as she was emerging from the kitchen.

He surveyed her work and then looked at her, surprise written all over his face.

'You don't waste time, do you?' He sounded impressed.

She sat at the table and looked at him without smiling. He didn't even have the decency to explain what had happened, just waltzed in as if nothing was wrong.

He came and sat at the table opposite her.

'You're annoyed with me, right?'

She tried to feign indifference. If that was the way he was going to treat her, then she'd treat him like a workman. That's what she had employed him as, wasn't it? And an unreliable one at that.

He took her silence as disapproval and stopped smiling.

'Sorry, something cropped up. I should have let you know. I'm sorry. Can I work for a couple of hours now to make up?'

He looked very drawn and not his usual self and she wondered if he had problems again.

'Yes, that's fine. I'm done for today. I need to catch up on my emails. You carry on as you wish. The sooner it's finished the better,' she said coldly.

He nodded and went to get the fork and wheelbarrow to shift the branches.

She tried not to watch him through the window as she sat at the dining table trying to concentrate on her messages. Even on holiday there was so much stuff from the office to deal with, but her eyes were constantly drawn to where he was heaving and chopping. She guessed he must be a little older than her, possibly in his late 30s and she wondered what the bad luck was that Elsie had talked about.

What was she thinking? He had no interest in her, that was clear. In ten days' time she'd be back in London. It would be good to be back in her flat and mixing in her own circle of friends. She had to forget all this silliness.

Rick cleared the heap of wood and then set to on the upper branches she hadn't been able to reach. He was working at twice the speed he usually did, not stopping to stretch and look around in his normal laid-back way, and soon had the lot piled up ready for his trailer. The garden was opening up all the time and she could now see the full extent of it. She hoped the size wouldn't put buyers off.

When he'd finished clearing all the wood away he popped his head round the door and said he'd be back again in

the morning. Then he was gone, leaving her feeling empty and hurt once again.

She needed to restock her food supply so went round to the village store early next morning. If Rick came he could get on without her. She felt like a walk and some company, even if it was only the village shopkeeper.

'You look a bit down,' Bel said as soon as she walked in. 'Country life a bit dull after the big lights?'

'Something like that. I'm worried about the cottage. It's in such a state I can't imagine anyone wanting it. I can't spend much time here getting it done up.'

Bel was sympathetic.

'Bet you wish your aunt hadn't lumbered you with it.'

'In a way. But to her it was her home and she probably felt she was leaving me all she had, which is true. I hate to seem ungrateful.'

Bel was serving Sally and introduced her as the barmaid from the pub.

'You ought to come in for a drink,' Sally said.

'Yes, I might,' Steph said, imagining Sally behind the bar with her blonde bobbed hair and broad smile. She could only be in her early 20s, but had exactly the right personality for the job she did.

'Don't be shy. We can have a chat. It's really friendly and nobody will think anything of you going in on your own.'

Steph felt a warm glow. That was nice. So she promised Sally that she would and meant it.

'Look, why don't you come round the back and I'll make us a cup of coffee? It's very quiet this morning and I'll hear the door if anyone comes in,' Bel offered.

The back room was small and untidy but homely, and Bel told her to sit down while she put on the kettle.

'How's the garden going? I hear Rick's helping you,' she called from the kitchen off the back room. Then she came through with two mugs and gave one to Steph.

'Yes, he's doing a good job. That's when he bothers to come.' Steph was

still disgruntled with him for messing her about.

'I suppose he's got a lot on at his place at this time of year. I'm surprised he's doing gardens at all just now.'

'What does he do, then?' Steph asked.

'Haven't you seen his market garden? You can't miss it. Boland's, the big place with all the greenhouses you see as you come into the village. That's Rick's place.'

She was shocked.

'Why does he do gardening for people if he's got that big place?'

'I think he just needs to get away sometimes. Gary and Mark are good workers, but not the sort Rick would choose for friends. It must be lonely for him in that bungalow all on his own. And he hates the work. It's not what he wants to do.'

'Why does he do it, then?' Steph asked.

Bel shrugged.

'He has to. No option, it seems.'

The shop door opened.

'Just my luck. No customers all morning, then when I make coffee they all come in.'

Bel went through to serve her customer, leaving Steph more mystified than ever. She sat drinking her coffee and thinking about what Bel had just told her. Why had Rick not mentioned it when she'd asked him what he did for a living? All he'd told her was that he did gardening and lived in the village. He'd never said he had a big market garden like that.

More customers came in and Steph waited impatiently for the shop to empty so she could quiz Bel a bit more. But there was no let up so in the end she felt she should go.

All the way home she thought about what Bel had said. It didn't make sense. Why had Rick been so secretive, letting her think he was just an odd-jobbing gardener when he had a place like that? Well, he obviously had his reasons and she wasn't going to pry. So long as he finished her garden, she'd just pay him and that was it.

He was hard at work clearing out the ditch.

'You'll have problems come winter if you don't get it cleared. It's full of rubbish.'

She shrugged.

'I'm not planning on being here in winter.' She was trying very hard to be business-like.

'No,' was all he said before returning to his work.

Steph had decided to continue with cleaning the house and keep out of his way. At about two o'clock Rick called in through the door that he was going and she tried not to mind.

An hour later he was back again with a pile of glass plate and a big grin on his face.

'Right, now we can re-glaze the greenhouse.'

She wasn't sure that was necessary. It looked OK now he'd taken the broken glass out and tidied it up. All she wanted was to get the place looking reasonable for sale.

He read her thoughts.

'Look, this lot didn't cost me anything and it would be a shame to take it down. It's a good solid frame.'

She felt uneasy accepting it, but couldn't think of any way of turning down such an offer without seeming ungrateful, especially as he looked so pleased with himself.

Within a couple of hours he'd managed to get most of the glass in place and had come into the kitchen to talk to her about some awkward bits he'd have to get cut to size when her phone rang. It was Greg.

'Just phoned to see how things are progressing,' he said. 'Are you sure you can't make it on Saturday?' he asked.

'Greg, I've told you I can't. I really am sorry. But I do have a lot to do.'

'I've checked on your flat. All seems fine. Oh, and there's a concert I'd like to go to next month. You'll be home for that, won't you?'

'Yes, that's fine.' That should pacify him.

When she put her phone down Rick was frowning.

'Boyfriend missing you?' he asked.

'No, not a boyfriend. Just a friend.'

'A friend you go to concerts with. A friend who keeps an eye on your flat.'

She didn't like the cynical tone in his voice.

'Yes, that's right. Anything wrong with that?'

He shrugged and turned to leave.

'Nothing at all.'

'Anyway, you shouldn't be listening in to my phone conversations,' she called after him.

He stopped at the door and looked back at her.

'Well, tell your boyfriend to keep his voice down. Everyone in the neighbourhood could hear him.' He gave a resigned shake of the head. 'I'll be off then.'

Rick was in a foul mood as he walked slowly back to Boland's. Steph obviously had something going with Greg.

He was blatantly more than a friend. He might have known a girl like Steph wouldn't be free and available. And what had he to offer in comparison? She was here for two weeks then off back to her fancy flat and her successful job and her circle of posh friends. He dug his hands deeper into his pockets and slouched back down the lane, peering at the ground ahead of him and wishing it would suck him down into its depths.

Steph watched him go and felt a pang of regret. Perhaps he really did care about her and she had deliberately ignored his feelings. He'd been so pleased with the greenhouse glass and enthusiastic about getting it done. Now Greg's call had wrecked everything.

Elsie came round later in the afternoon to see how things were progressing, and was surprised by what she saw.

'My, you've done miracles. And the garden's beginning to look a treat. Rose would be right pleased with it. She always kept it so nice until the rheumatics got to her.'

Steph sighed.

'I wish I'd come to see her more.'

'Now, don't you go feeling bad. Thought a lot of you, she did. Was proud as punch when you wrote and told her about your qualifications and the job you were doing. Said she'd always known you were a bright spark.'

Steph smiled. She could just see Rose reading her letters and then telling everyone how clever her niece was.

She made Elsie some tea and they sat outside, but Steph couldn't get the mystery of Rick out of her mind. She didn't want Elsie jumping to the wrong conclusion so she simply mentioned what Bel had told her about him not liking working at Boland's and hoped Elsie would expand on it.

'My, lass, it's a long story. I feel right sorry for that young man. He's a good lad. Nothing's too much trouble for him. But the way he's been treated, it's not right.'

Elsie shook her head but didn't continue, and Steph felt she couldn't press her for more information without arousing suspicion. Anyway, they shouldn't be discussing him at all. She had no business prying into village affairs that had nothing to do with her, so she changed the subject.

Greg phoned that evening and again tried to persuade her to come back home.

'I really miss you,' he told her.

It was reassuring to know someone cared about her, someone she could trust and who wouldn't mess her about.

'Things are going well here now, so I might make the barbecue after all,' she told him.

This cheered him up and he filled her in on all the happenings she was missing by being away. She listened contentedly while sitting at the open kitchen door, watching a blackbird digging for worms in the newly turned soil.

On Friday the survey arrived with the morning post. It didn't make pleasant reading and she got on to Bradley immediately to discuss her options. She couldn't see how she was going to sell the place with a survey like this.

Bradley did nothing to dispel her fears.

'We've had properties like yours on our books for years,' he told her. 'It really would help if you could put some of this right.'

There was no way she could do that. Her finances were stretched to the limit already.

More depressed than ever, she decided to make a start on Rose's bedroom. She hadn't been able to face up to that yet, but things couldn't get much worse today so she might as well do something useful. It was depressing work. Rose had very little in the way of clothes and they were old fashioned and well worn. Her dressing table had only a jar of hand cream and some hairpins and a hair brush. There were a couple of pairs of smart shoes that didn't look as if they'd been worn. She must have lived in the old flat ones by the back door.

Rick didn't show up, which didn't surprise her as she now knew he was just fitting her in when he needed a change of scenery. In fact, after today's news she wondered if it was worth continuing with the garden. By the time the place was sold it would all be a wilderness again.

Closing Rose's bedroom door she went into her own bedroom and, with only a brief look in the mirror to tidy a few escaped strands of hair, she strode purposefully out of the cottage. It wasn't far to the market garden that Bel had told her about. Now she knew where he lived she'd go and tell him not to bother coming anymore.

The fresh air was welcome after the dusty cottage and she strode out and breathed deeply. As it came into view she took in the details she hadn't noticed when passing it before. There were greenhouses, a couple of fields of something leafy growing, some barns and sheds, a large brick bungalow in the centre and an accumulation of farming vehicles lined up at the side. There was a big sign saying *Boland's Produce* at the end of the drive leading up to the barn.

Feeling a little intimidated by it all she slowed her pace and cautiously ventured round the hedge, trying to see if she could spot him. Knocking on that door didn't seem like a good idea anymore. She turned and made her way back as quickly as she could.

Back in the safety of her cottage she got on with her sorting. Rick would turn up eventually and then she could tell him not to bother coming again.

Fed up, she made her way though the bin liners full of paper to answer a rather persistent knocking at the back door, and was delighted to see Sally standing there.

'I'm going into Southport for the afternoon and thought you might enjoy a change of scenery,' she said. 'It's my afternoon off.'

'You're a star,' Steph told her. 'Give me five minutes to clean up and you're on.'

They had a lovely afternoon. There was no mention of Rick, and Steph wasn't going to bring up the subject. It was refreshing to wander round the shops and forget all about him. She bought a summer dress, some white trousers, sandals and a pretty top. Then they went into a café and had afternoon tea. It was all so pleasant, chatting about everything, laughing a lot, and Steph felt she had known Sally for ever.

She'd only been back in the cottage a few minutes when Rick arrived.

'Caught you at last. Where have you been all day?' he inquired.

'Shopping with Sally.' She kicked her shoes off and he followed her into the kitchen and stood watching her fill the kettle.

'I have something for you,' he said. He looked a little sheepish. 'Sorry about before. I shouldn't have reacted the way I did. Will you forgive me?'

She was too happy to be cross with him.

'Go on, then. So what have you got me?'

He went to his truck and she watched through the front window as he took out several boxes of plants and carried them round the side of the house. Then she opened the back door to see what he was doing.

He put the boxes on the ground then turned to her.

'You said you wanted colour in those tubs so I've brought you some plants. I thought we could put them in together.'

The boxes were full of geraniums and other plants she didn't recognise.

Seeing her hesitate he explained.

'They don't look much at the moment, but once they start flowering they'll give a lovely show.'

She pushed her feet into the sandals by the kitchen door and went out to join him. How could she be cross with him when he'd been so thoughtful?

When they'd finished they sat and

admired their work and she felt a great sense of satisfaction. The sun was dipping low behind the hedge and the air was cool and fresh. It was a lovely evening and she wasn't going to spoil it with questions and incriminations. He'd been upset by Greg's phone call because he cared about her. Rick had apologised and brought the plants as a peace offering. If he wanted to tell her about his life, he would. Otherwise, whatever was going on was his own business. He stayed to have a glass of wine with her and they watched the sunset colour the sky scarlet.

When he got up to go he hesitated.

'It's the village show on Saturday. I'm showing some of my produce. I won second for my tomatoes last year.' He gave an embarrassed smile. 'It must seem silly to you, but that's village life.' He shrugged.

'I'll be there. Wouldn't miss it for the world.'

'Great. It's fun.' His smile became more natural, but he still seemed a little tense as he stood there, reluctant to go. 'They have a disco in the village hall afterwards. Bit of a bun fight, but we all go. Will you come to that, too?'

She hesitated. Going to look around a tent of prize marrows was one thing. Walking into a dance on her own was entirely different. Rick noticed and read her mind.

'I'll be tied up all day helping with this and that, but I have no duties in the evening so I'll pick you up and we can go together. Would you like that?'

Her heart was doing somersaults.

'Yes, I would. Thank you.'

He didn't say anything and she smiled up at him and their eyes met. He relaxed.

'Great, I think you'll enjoy it. Oh, and they do a hog roast so don't eat beforehand.' With that he ambled off.

A Trip Down Memory Lane

Saturday was definitely going to be a day off from all the sorting, cleaning and gardening. Steph wasn't even going to open her laptop, but have a lie in, a good long soak in the bath and then put on something nice to go along to the village hall. In fact, the sun dress and sandals she'd bought in Southport would be perfect. She was really looking forward to a bit of village life.

It was a lovely day and when she arrived at the hall at two o'clock the show was in full swing. Tables had been set out on the village green and there was a big marquee for the exhibits. She wandered around looking at everything and eventually found Rick's tomatoes. He had come first in his section and Jim was second. But Jim had won with his marrow and Elsie had a second for her flower arrangement.

When she'd seen everything and had her fill of cakes and tea, she went back to the cottage to prepare for the evening. A mixture of excitement and panic alternated and she couldn't make up her mind whether she was looking forward to the evening or dreading it.

Rick had said he would take her, but would he stay with her or would she be left on her own while everyone else was in pairs? She could always sit with Sally and Bel and get to know some more of the village folk. So she shrugged off the uncertain feeling and changed into the white trousers and top she'd bought in Southport with Sally, determined to enjoy whatever the evening presented.

Rick picked her up as promised, took her to the hall and never left her side all evening. They joined Sally and Bel at a table near the doorway with some of Rick's friends and he made sure he sat beside her. When the music stopped for refreshments all the children poured on to the floor in a noisy riot and Rick took her hand and led her outside to queue up for some of the roast.

It was a perfect evening, balmy with a golden sky and a slight breeze wafting the trees. They sat on the grass and ate, then wandered round while Rick introduced her to people she hadn't met and they were all friendly and interested in her cottage.

When they heard the music start up again they went back into the hall. Everyone was on the floor doing whatever they fancied to the party tunes they were playing. She joined in and found it all relaxing and fun. Rick was acting the goat and doing the most ridiculous steps to the music and everyone was laughing and clapping him.

Then everything slowed down and the music became slow and dreamy. Couples were forming to dance a slow number so Steph turned to walk from the floor but Rick caught up with her and took her arm.

'Where are you off to?' he asked.

She shrugged and he took her in his arms and began to move to the music.

It was wonderful to have his arms round her and she felt she could never be happier than she was at that moment. He was a good dancer and held her firmly as he guided her round the floor amongst the other couples. As they danced he pulled her closer to him and their steps became slower until they were just moving to the rhythm and holding each other.

She'd never felt like this before as she melted into his arms, wishing the music never to stop. He smelled of aftershave and something she couldn't put a name to. When the music stopped they clung together until he turned her and guided her from the floor. They hadn't said a word. It would have spoiled the moment.

Back at the table she noticed a few strange looks and knew she was blushing, but Rick ignored them and still held her hand. Then the music started again and it was another noisy party dance.

'Let's go outside for a bit of air,' he whispered in her ear. She was hot and glad to escape the looks, so agreed.

They walked round the green and into the parkland surrounding it, enjoying the cool evening air. Rick put an arm around her shoulder and she looked up at him.

'Are you all right?' he asked.

'Never better.' she said and was rewarded with one of his lovely smiles.

When they went back into the hall the dancing was in riotous swing again with everyone on the floor. Then she noticed Bel had moved to one of the other tables and she looked away when Steph caught her eye. Rick left her to attend to some problem with one of the loudspeakers and as she sat down Sally came over and sat beside her.

'Glad you came?' Sally asked.

'Yes, absolutely. It's great fun.'

They chatted for a while then Steph caught a glimpse of Bel leaving the hall. She looked really miserable.

'What's wrong with Bel?' Steph asked Sally.

Sally gave her a strange look and said nothing.

'What's wrong?' she asked again, feeling there was something she was missing here.

Sally pulled a face and seemed reluctant to go on. Then she said, 'Oh, don't worry about it. She sometimes gets into these moods. She'll get over it. Now, let's get on that floor. I can't sit still when they play this tune.'

She dragged Steph on to the floor again and soon they were jumping around and laughing like a couple of teenagers. She caught sight of Rick standing on the stage looking at her, smiling and shaking his head, which made her more determined to give him something to laugh about. She was in one of her silly moods and enjoying herself immensely.

When the disco finally packed up Steph helped pile the chairs and stack the tables. All the rubbish was gathered into bin liners and left by the door and everyone filtered out into the cool of the night.

Rick put an arm round her and

guided her to the car.

'What a great evening,' she said. 'I can't remember when I enjoyed myself more.'

He squeezed a little tighter.

'I'm glad. I wanted you to enjoy this evening. You've worked and worried about that cottage all week. You deserved a break.'

They gave Elsie and Jim a lift home and then Rick dropped Steph off at the cottage and kissed her gently on the cheek and drove off. She felt a little disappointed but went in happy. It really had been a lovely day.

But she worried about why Bel had acted so strangely, going home early, and the way Sally had reacted. Bel hadn't struck her as the moody type. But she was too tired to worry about it tonight, and as soon as she was in bed she drifted into a peaceful sleep.

She was well into the second week of her holiday now. The garden was looking good. The flowers Rick had brought were beginning to bloom and she liked them. This gardening business was getting into her bones. But soon someone else would be making the decisions when they bought the place, not her.

Rick hadn't been for days now and she was trying hard not to let it disturb her. He'd been so attentive and warm at the village disco and she had been taken in by his attention. It was quite ridiculous the way she was behaving. She'd had a lovely evening with Rick and the others and nothing could change that.

She was sitting outside with her morning coffee and thinking she might take the afternoon off for another shopping trip when he ambled round the side of the cottage wearing a short sleeved shirt and beige cords, not the scruffy jeans and T-shirt he wore when working. But his smile was the same and his eyes as warm as always.

'Coffee?' she offered, trying to make it sound casual, even though her heart had given a lurch of pleasure at seeing him again. She was not going to let anything he did or say upset her from now on.

He perched on the seat opposite as she sat down again.

'Going somewhere nice?' she said to fill in the silence.

'I hope so,' he replied.

She shrugged, trying to keep a check on her disappointment.

'OK, what's the damages, then?' She assumed he had come to give her his bill and pick up his tools.

'There are no damages, at least I hope not,' he said, smiling.

She was flustered.

'No, I mean what do I owe you?'

'I know what you mean and you owe me nothing.'

'But I do. I insist. You've done a good job.'

'We've done a good job.' he corrected her.

'OK, I helped, yes. But it is my cottage and you put in all those hours of hard work.'

He leaned across the table and took her hand. It felt warm and reassuring and she didn't pull away. She didn't avert her eyes as his held her gaze.

'I've enjoyed doing it. It's been a tonic to me. A change from my normal humdrum job. To see this garden take shape and be restored to what it was when Rose took care of it has been payment enough. It's all the reward I need.'

She was melting in those eyes and wished he would hold her hand for ever. She felt she could cope with anything if she had this man beside her, supporting her, loving her. Then she shook herself. It wasn't going to happen. They came from different worlds. In four days' time she would be on the motorway, speeding back to reality.

He squeezed her hand a little tighter and his voice was low, a little uncertain.

'What I was wondering was, if we could have a day out together, to celebrate the transformation of the garden, where would you like to go?' he asked.

She thought about it. Yes, she knew exactly where she wanted to go. She released his hand, jumped up and stood before him, grinning like an excited child.

'Would you mind terribly if we took a trip down memory lane? I'd love to stand outside my old school again and romp on the sand dunes at Ainsdale. I'd like to walk through the pine woods at Formby and hunt for red squirrels as I used to as a child. And then I want to go on to Crosby and see those Anthony Gormley statues on the beach. I've seen them on TV and they look amazing.'

He leaned back, a look of mock horror on his face.

'That's some day out. You don't do thing by halves, do you?'

Her smile faded and she felt stupid. He was probably only suggesting a pub lunch or something.

'Sorry.' She shrugged, looking down at the table.

But he'd stood up and was jangling his car keys.

'Come on, then. If we're to get through that schedule, we'd better make a start.'

When she met his eyes they held amusement and an enthusiasm to match her own and her joy returned. A vision crossed her mind of Greg in the same situation. He would have sighed and said he had something more important to do, and perhaps she could do it with a girl friend some time.

As they sped along the country lanes out of the village she wondered again about Rick's life. He'd asked her lots of questions about her life so why shouldn't she ask a few? Now seemed like a good time.

'What is your work? I mean, other than gardening for people?' She thought it best to pretend she had no idea what he did, rather than to let him know that she and Bel had been talking about him.

He tightened his grip on the wheel

and she immediately wished she'd kept her mouth shut. It was a while before he replied and his voice was carefully controlled.

'I work at Boland's, the big market garden just outside the village.'

So he didn't own it, after all. He just worked there. Not the impression Bel had given.

'I've seen it. It's huge. So why the gardening? I'd have thought you'd have had enough of it there.' She tried to keep her tone from being prying.

Again the long pause.

'That's not gardening. It's not what I want to do. It's just a job and it's where I live.'

She wanted to keep him talking, find out more.

'I think I'd look for something else if I was that fed up with my job. We spend too much time working not to enjoy it. What is it you want to do?'

'Landscape gardening or working on a big estate. Work I'm trained for, what I spent three years at college to learn.

It's why I do people's gardens. It's satisfying. You see real results. All I get at Boland's is rows and rows of lettuces and endless greenhouses full of tomatoes for lorries to cart away and sell. It's soul-destroying work.'

'What's stopping you, then?'

'It's complicated.' He turned momentarily and smiled at her, but it held a weight of sorrow and she knew she mustn't delve further.

As they approached the town he turned to her.

'Now, where exactly is this old school of yours?'

He seemed back on form again and she pushed any misgivings out of her mind. What did it matter about any complications in his life? She had this gorgeous man for the day and she was going to make the best of it.

'Just carry on along Rotten Row. I want to see all the lovely flowers. It used to look a treat in the summer. I remember walking along in a crocodile all the way from school to the playing

75

field for hockey.'

It didn't disappoint, so they stopped the car and ambled along the beautifully laid out beds of flowers. Rick was in his element, commenting on every bloom, and she understood why growing tomatoes and lettuce wasn't quite the same.

When they'd had their fill of the colourful displays they went back to the car and he followed her directions down a few side streets and, parking where she told him, they got out.

'No school here as far as I can see.' Rick looked bemused, and she was puzzled as she stared through a set of big iron gates at the large old house within them.

'That was my school,' she said in a dull voice.

He stood beside her and shook his head in disbelief.

'This was your school? It's a block of very exclusive flats now.'

'I can see that.'

He turned her to face him.

'I can't believe this!'

'Why not? I'm telling you that was my school. I went there for five years so I should know.'

'I believe you, because I remember when these flats went up for sale. You're not going to believe what I'm going to tell you.'

'What?'

'Do you want to go into your old school and see what they've done with it?'

She shook her head.

'We can't do that. There are people living there now.'

He was laughing.

'Do you want to go inside?'

She shook her head in exasperation, but he took her hand and pressed some numbers into the pad in the side wall. The gates swung open. They walked up the curving drive, past the old cycle sheds and, once they were standing inside the arched front entrance on the cold stone steps, he keyed in some more numbers on the pad outside the enormous front door. Her heart was thumping. What was he up to?

'It's OK.' He laughed at her face. 'My father lives here. Come on or he'll wonder what's kept us.'

It was, without doubt, an upmarket flat. Rick's father was a tall handsome man in his late 60s and Steph immediately liked him. He had silver grey hair and a twinkle in his eye she couldn't resist. He took her hand and kissed it very gallantly then patted Rick's arm and said how nice it was to see him. Rick explained about the school and who Steph was and why they were there.

'It's a very nice flat,' Steph said, taking in the spacious room, with sash windows, tasteful decor and furnishings.

'Used to be the head teacher's quarters,' his father told her. 'Fancy you going to school here. It must have been tiny for a school.'

Steph was just about catching her breath and taking it all in.

'Yes, I suppose it was. But private schools often are. It was a lovely place to come to. We had fires in the classrooms and sat round tables with the teachers in the dining-room for lunch like one big family.' She smiled. 'Could you imagine that now?'

His father smiled at her.

'I'm glad they didn't destroy its character when they converted it into flats. But then, it was a large house before it became a school, I believe.'

He turned to Rick.

'This is a pleasant surprise. Thought you would have been working today. Not turned you out, has she?'

'Dad, can we leave it, please? We have a guest.'

His father looked at him in a resigned way that made Steph wonder what it was all about. Then he turned back to her with a smile.

'Forgive me, my dear. I'm being rude. But I see my son so rarely these days that I have to make the best of it and catch up on his news. Now, shall I make us a cup of tea?'

Steph was about to accept when Rick interrupted.

'No, Dad, we're on our way to Formby. Steph wants to find some red squirrels. We only came in because she wanted to see her old school again.'

He seemed a little disappointed but made no objection.

'Well, just let me show you something before you rush off,' he said to Steph and led her into a small study. 'Now, what do you think about that?'

In a corner Steph saw a small wooden desk and gasped.

'That's my old desk!' she shrieked.

Rick's father laughed.

'Well, I doubt it, but it could have been. When I bought the flat they had a sale of the old school furniture. I bought it as a bit of nostalgia, but never used it and it means little to me.' His smile became indulgent. 'Why don't you have it? I've often wondered why I bought it. It just takes up room. Would you like it, Steph?'

Steph didn't know what to make of the offer.

'Take it,' Rick told her. 'Dad's right, it only gets in the way. I'll pick it up for you in the morning and bring it round to the cottage.'

Steph was delighted with the gift and said how much it would mean to her. They said goodbye and left.

When they got back to the car Rick put an arm round her shoulder.

'So what do you make of your old school? Are you disappointed?' he asked.

Steph smiled back.

'No, not really. It felt strange, but everything changes. It was nice meeting your father. He seems like a lovely man. It was very kind of him to give the desk to me.'

'He liked you. Next time we'll stay longer. Only today we have a lot to do.'

So there was going to be a next time. Her spirits lightened. Rick was so like his dad, with the same lovely smile and a twinkle in his eye. She'd never felt like this about anyone before, not even Simon.

For the rest of the day she was very cautious. Why had his dad said that about him being 'turned out'? And why did Rick stop him saying more?

They didn't see any red squirrels, but had great fun chasing each other up and down the sand dunes. She was a child again; young, happy, carefree. As she came tumbling down one she lost her footing and Rick caught her at the bottom and, pulling her into his arms, kissed her very gently on the mouth. It took her by surprise, but she offered no resistance and as the kiss progressed into something much deeper, she relaxed and melted into the moment.

It was late evening when they got to Crosby and she found herself mesmerised by the statues on Crosby beach — a hundred life-size figures sculpted in cast iron dotted irregularly on the sand and staring out to sea. They strolled hand in hand along the wet sand, studying each in turn.

As the sun lowered over the horizon and the sky turned scarlet, the statues became silhouettes looking out to sea in an eerie landscape. They clung together in silent wonder and then Rick kissed her again and the world receded.

They got some fish and chips on the way home and ate them on the beach in the moonlight. Then he drove her back to the cottage and kissed her lightly on the cheek before she got out of the car. Letting herself in through the front door, she couldn't have been happier.

An Unsettling Turn
of Events

Steph's happiness was short lived. It was late the following afternoon when there was a sharp rapping on the door and a heavy-looking woman about her own age with a sour face framed with dull, straight hair stood outside and thrust a piece of paper into her hand.

'I've brought your bill,' she said. 'He had no business taking that greenhouse glass. It will have to be paid for.'

Steph stared at the worn jeans and grubby sweater and wondered who she was. She looked at the bill then back at the woman.

'I'm sorry, but I don't know who you are.'

'Maybe not. Rick tends to forget these small details.'

'Well, I certainly don't want anything

for nothing and I'll sort this out with him next time I see him.'

Steph waited for the woman to go but she didn't.

'Well, are you going to settle or not?'

'No, not until I see Rick. My business is with him and I will make sure he gets paid,' she said.

The woman looked undecided, then said, 'Make sure you do.' And she walked back down the path and through the gate without looking back.

Steph was shaking all over. How could Rick have done this to her? Who was that woman? She slumped on to the chair and stared into space in a daze.

When the shaking had stopped and she began to think more clearly, she knew she had to find out more, and the only person who would help her was Elsie.

Jim opened the door, a worried look on his face.

'Oh, lass, come in. I'm right glad to see you.'

'What's wrong?' she asked.

He led her through into the kitchen where Elsie was sitting, pale faced, with a pack of frozen peas on her ankle.

'She were up on the stool and took a tumble,' Jim explained.

'Aye, it's nought. Don't fuss. Bit of a sprain, I reckon. Now put the kettle on and make me and Steph a cup of tea.'

Jim obeyed, relieved to be told what to do while Steph examined the ankle.

'I think you're right, Elsie,' she told her. 'But it does look swollen. Have you any bandages? That might help.'

Jim found the first-aid box and Steph bound the ankle firmly with a crêpe bandage.

'My, that feels grand. You've done that before, I see.'

Steph laughed.

'I did first aid at school. Never thought it would come in handy, though.'

Jim left them to their tea and went back into the garden to finish cutting the grass, relieved to be let off the hook for a while.

As Steph sipped her tea the feeling of panic returned.

'Elsie, I want to ask you something.'

Elsie listened while she told her about the incident. When she burst into tears, Elsie reached forward as best she could and patted her arm.

'Aye, lass, don't take on now. She had no business talking to you like that. Rick's a good man as'll do anything for anyone. So don't you start thinking otherwise. He's got his self into a bit of a tight corner and no mistake.'

Elsie winced and tried to get her leg more comfortable, but the pain seemed to be causing her a lot of distress.

'Do you have any pain killers?' Steph asked, wiping her eyes on a tissue.

'I've some in that cupboard,' she said, pointing to a big cupboard at the far end of the kitchen. It was a shambles of packets and tins and all sorts of bits and pieces, and it took Steph some time to find what she was looking for. By the time she'd filled a tumbler with water and given it to

Elsie, the pain seemed to have subsided somewhat. But Elsie looked drawn and tired.

'I think I'll lie back a bit and rest,' she said.

'Are you sure you'll be all right?' Steph asked, adjusting the stool under Elsie's bad leg.

'Yes, dear. Now you go off home, and don't you worry about that young man. He'll sort it all out for you.'

Steph had no idea what she was talking about, but as Elsie's eyes were closing she thought it best to leave her in peace. So she went out and had a word with Jim, who was now in his shed fixing a chair leg that had come loose.

'I'll go back in now and sit with her,' he said.

'Let me know if you're worried,' Steph told him. 'I'll drive you to the hospital.'

He thanked her and Steph left.

She felt calmer now and was glad she hadn't said more. She didn't want Elsie becoming suspicious about her feelings for Rick, especially the way gossip spread round this village. The best thing was to leave it. She'd broken all her own rules and trusted a man again and deserved all she got.

She wasn't ready to go back to the cottage. She was too worked up, so she walked on past the cottage towards the village. She would make her way out towards the open marsh and the sea. The solitude there would help soothe her before she turned in for the night. She'd often walked there as a child when she wanted some solitude. It was a peaceful place.

The pub seemed quiet as she glanced in through the door, and she saw Sally polishing glasses behind the bar. It looked warm and inviting, and Sally had suggested she come in some time. Now seemed like as good a time as any, and she could do with some congenial company.

Sally was pleased to see her.

'What a nice surprise! You look as if you need a drink. Bad day?'

'You could say that. As if I haven't enough problems with the cottage, I now have some dreadful woman accusing me of stealing her greenhouse glass.'

Sally frowned.

'That'll be Fiona. I heard she's back. Big trouble, that one. Always has been. Don't know how a decent bloke like Rick ever got involved with her.'

Steph perched on a bar stool and Sally put some wine in front of her. She emptied half the glass then sat cradling the rest in her hands. Sally noticed and put down the glass she was polishing.

'What's this about greenhouse glass? She only came back today.'

Steph looked up at Sally.

'Rick's been doing my garden and she obviously wasn't happy about it. It was Elsie's idea. I thought he did that sort of thing for a living. Nobody put me in the picture. Then this happens.' She took another gulp at her wine and nearly emptied the glass.

Sally shook her head.

'I bet you'll be glad to get back to

London, won't you?'

Steph sighed.

'Actually, no. I like it here. Except when I get accused of doing something I haven't done.'

Sally laughed.

'I wouldn't worry about it if I were you. Her bark's worse than her bite.'

'Who is she, anyway?'

A customer came in through the door and Sally hesitated.

'Look, I can't explain now,' she said, then went to serve him.

Steph slowly sipped what was left of her wine and Sally refilled her glass. There were several men coming in now, obviously finished work and wanting a pint before settling down for the evening.

Sally kept chatting to her and introduced her to the regulars at the bar, but there was no more opportunity for serious conversation. They were a friendly lot and some remembered her from the dance. Any more information from Sally was out of the question, so she slowly sipped her wine and absorbed the cordial atmosphere.

'Trouble's back,' one of the men said to Sally.

'What she come back for? Thought she'd gone for good,' another said.

Steph tensed. Talking in confidence with Sally about it was one thing, but this general gossip made her feel uncomfortable and she hoped none of them had heard of what had happened to her that afternoon.

Then the talk suddenly stopped and an uncomfortable quiet gradually gave way to more general remarks about the weather. Rick had come into the pub and was now standing in the doorway looking round.

He spotted her and quickly looked away. One of the regulars called him over but he didn't respond. After a minute or two, he backed out.

Steph sat rigid. This whole thing was getting out of hand. All she wanted to do now was get back to London and leave it behind her. The cottage would sell one day, and if it didn't she couldn't help it. She hadn't asked for any of this. She wanted her life back.

She finished her drink and eased herself off the bar stool and made her way outside. It was a beautiful moonlit night and the fresh air was welcome as she ambled slowly in the direction of the cottage.

Rick was waiting outside in his car. He followed her into the cottage looking like thunder. She tried to ignore him, knowing that to stop him coming in with her would only cause a scene on the lane and she preferred to have her disputes in private.

She put on the light over the television and went to her bag, took out her cheque book and, with a shaking hand, wrote out a cheque for the amount Fiona had requested. He stood quite still, watching her. When she handed it to him he took it and ripped it to pieces in front of her, letting the bits fall to the ground.

'She had no right to come here,' Rick said.

'No,' Steph agreed, and as their eyes met in the dim light, the anger seemed to drain away from him. 'Steph, I'm sorry. What more can I say?'

'Nothing at all,' she said quietly, not giving way to the compassion she felt. 'You've made a fool out of me and I don't like people doing that.'

'Steph, will you listen to me, please?'

'No, there is nothing you can say that will make any of what happened today any better. If you don't want paying that's your problem, but tell that woman not to come here again.' She was fighting to keep her composure when every fibre of her being wanted to reach out and take away his hurt.

He stood stiffly; his brow creased, his mouth tight, his tone measured.

'I didn't know she was coming back, and I certainly would have stopped her coming here if I'd known.'

She turned away.

'It doesn't matter.'

He pulled her back towards him in agitation.

'It does matter.'

He was talking faster now.

'When I got in from the bank at lunchtime she was there. She was asking Gary why he was loading stones into the truck. They were for your pond. I thought they'd look good round the edge. Then she spotted some broken panes of glass at the bottom and wanted to know about that, too. We had a row and she stormed out. I thought she was just going off to cool down. I had no idea she was coming here.'

He was getting worked up and she didn't want to hear any more. She didn't know who the woman was, and she didn't want to. It would be too painful. She'd heard all the explanations before, from a time she was trying desperately to put out of her mind. All she wanted now was to get him out of her cottage and shut the door and be left in peace with her hurt and pain.

'Please leave,' she whispered. 'I really can't deal with this. Please go.'

Rick had drained of all colour.

'It's not what you think, Steph.'

'I don't know what I think. Please don't say any more.'

He stood looking at her, not knowing what to say or do, lost in his own misery. He slowly and uncertainly left. She watched him go then closed the door, drained of emotion.

Rick stood outside in the lane and wondered what he should do. He'd never seen Steph like that before and it scared him. He wanted to explain, to reassure her that Fiona was in his past. He wanted to take her in his arms and tell her how much he loved her. But she wouldn't let him near and, while her voice was measured, there was a look of hurt in her eyes that tore at his heart.

He knew what she was feeling; that he'd deceived her and let her down. He began to walk. He needed to think, to get away, find another job. Tomorrow he would start looking, and the further away from here the better.

★　★　★

First thing next morning Steph phoned Greg and told him she would be back on Saturday. There was no point in hanging around. He was pleased she was coming home and that they could go to Greta's barbecue together, and this made her feel better. Once she was away from here things would go back to normal. She had a busy week ahead of her at work and this village would soon recede into memory.

Bel was in the shop on her own unpacking an order when Steph went in for some coffee. She continued in silence, only saying a curt hello in response to Steph's, and remained stony faced when she took her money. Steph was at a loss as to why she was being treated like this. She tried to make conversation, but Bel didn't respond, and as soon as she'd given her the change she disappeared into the back room leaving Steph alone in the shop.

Not prepared to go after her, Steph left the shop feeling deeply troubled.

Bel had been so friendly and nice to her. So why was she behaving like this?

She couldn't settle to anything for the rest of the day. Her mind was all over the place. How had she upset Bel? Why had she turned Rick away when he had done nothing wrong, and had come round to see her to put things right? All he had ever done was help her with the garden and take her on enjoyable outings. If she had read more into it then that was her fault. He wasn't responsible for that awful woman's behaviour, and he had cared enough to come round and see her.

That evening, just as she was washing up after her meal, Sally came round with a bottle of wine.

'How did you know I wanted that?' she asked in amazement.

'I didn't,' Sally said. 'I needed a bit of convivial company and thought who better than my new best friend?'

Steph wiped a tear that was threatening to run down her cheek and smiled weakly.

'Wow, you do need it,' Sally said, and put an arm round her shoulder. 'Come on, girl, get this bottle opened.'

Steph found the corkscrew and poured two glasses.

'So what's it all about? That Fiona hasn't been upsetting you again, has she?' Sally said.

'No, not really. It's more than that.'

'It's Rick, then?'

'So what have you heard now?' Steph was getting resigned to the fact that in this village nothing stayed private for long.

'I hear most things. Goes with the job, I'm afraid. First of all Bel, then you. That man's got a lot to answer for.' She laughed.

'What about Bel? What do you mean?' Steph asked.

Sally raised an eyebrow.

'Had her eye on him for ages now. They get on really well, do Bel and Rick. But she doesn't stand a chance with that one always coming back and causing trouble. And now you're on the scene. Poor old Bel.'

'What, you mean Bel and Rick are an item?'

'It's nothing like that. In fact, I think it's rather one sided; she's reading more into it than she should. Rick's nice to everyone. But Bel's got it into her head that some day the two of them will get together.'

'I had no idea,' Steph said. 'So now I'm the bad guy. I bet everyone will think I'm waltzing in here and making trouble and then I'll disappear again. They must hate me.'

'Don't be daft. They like a good gossip round here, that's for sure, but they don't hate you. In fact, from what I've heard, most people feel a bit sorry for you with this cottage to sort out and you living so far away.'

So everyone was talking about her. Hate her or feel sorry for her — which was worse?

'At least I know now why Bel's been cold towards me. She hardly spoke to me when I went in the shop. It's about the dance, isn't it?'

Sally shrugged.

'Well, he did spend all evening with you. I expect Bel was hoping for a dance with him herself. But I wouldn't worry. She'll get over it.'

'But I didn't realise what the situation was. I'm just an outsider here and I don't want to upset people. I wish someone had told me. Surely Rick must have realised how she would feel.'

'You know what he's like. He's done a brilliant job on your garden. He does a lot round the village to help people. He offered to do it for Rose, but she'd always had such a pride in her garden she couldn't admit that she couldn't do it herself anymore. He's always nice to everyone.'

Steph wasn't listening anymore. All she could think about was how hurt Bel must feel and how she must resent her coming to the village and attracting so much attention from the man she loved. She knew exactly how Bel felt.

Rick was nice to everyone and it

meant nothing. She and Bel were in the same boat. She wanted to talk to Bel about it, to share some of the pain, but she couldn't think of a way without embarrassing her or making it sound as if she was patronising her or feeling sorry for her.

'Am I talking to myself?' Sally said.

'Sorry. I'm confused. I didn't know how Bel felt. And who is this Fiona everyone's talking about?'

'Oh, my goodness, girl, you are out of it. She's his ex-wife. She left Rick years ago and went off to Ormskirk with this chap, Steve. Poor old Rick was in a state.'

'So, why's she back?'

'S'pose she's left Steve. She seems to have moved back into Boland's and Rick's moved out. I don't know how they're going to sort things out.'

'But she can't just waltz back after all this time, surely.'

'Well, yes, I think she can. It's her place, you see. Her father owned it and when he died it became hers. Rick stayed and carried on the business when Fiona left, but now she's back he can't stop her living there. It's a big business now, thanks to Rick's efforts, but madam there won't see it that way. What an awful situation.'

Steph felt more depressed than ever. The wine was having the opposite effect to the one she hoped it would have.

'So where's Rick living now?'

'I think he's staying with his father, but he's still running the place as far as I know. Fiona couldn't manage without him. They'll sort something out eventually, I expect. I wouldn't get too involved if I was you. Now, tell me what's happening with the cottage.'

'Still no sale,' Steph said.

'That why you're all wound up?'

'I expect so.'

'Well, it'll go eventually. Golly, everyone seems to have problems at the moment. Makes my life seem like a piece of cake.'

After Sally had gone, Steph kept turning it over in her mind until she hardly knew what to think or feel. Rick had been married; Fiona was his ex-wife. Now he was in this awful situation. What would he do? He worked at Boland's and it was his home. He couldn't live with his father for ever. How could he and Fiona work together after all this time?

She resolved to keep her head down and not get involved with anyone in the village again until she left for home on Saturday. It was too complicated and would end in hurt. There was plenty to keep her occupied here in the cottage, masses of work to catch up on from the office and a pile of stuff to read.

Eventually she went to bed. Her head ached and, though she felt drained, she knew she wouldn't sleep.

Back to Reality

On Friday morning there was a phone call from Bradley with someone wanting to look round the cottage. She quickly tidied it and felt quite optimistic. It really looked nice and cosy now, and the garden did look cared for.

Ken and Nora Barnes were a middle-aged couple who seemed to like what they saw.

'Aye, you've done wonders with it,' Ken said. 'I saw it last year and you wouldn't think it was the same place.'

Nora was interested in the garden.

'Now there's a proper garden,' she enthused.

'Have you seen the surveyor's report?' Steph asked tentatively. She didn't want them getting carried away and then realising what they were taking on.

'Oh, aye. I knew it were in need of attention. Like I said, I were here last year to see to the roof. But it's nought I can't fix.'

'He can fix ought, can our Ken,' Nora said. 'Been in building trade all his life, he has.'

They poked around for what seemed a very long time, deciding what was to be done, and then left with the promise to be in touch.

After they'd gone she went to the window and stared out. The garden did look good. She turned and looked round the room. It was cosy. She was seeing it through their eyes. They liked it. They might even buy it.

A deep feeling of emptiness settled on her and she sank on to the kitchen chair and rested her head on her arms on the table. Could she really go home and forget all about Rick and the good times they'd spent together and the companionship they'd shared in the garden? Could her life return to what it had been in London? She doubted it, but she had to try. There was no alternative.

But there was one thing she had to do before she went home tomorrow. She had to see Bel and sort out this misunderstanding. It would be difficult, and she dreaded it, but she had never been one to shirk her duty.

She pulled a cardigan over her blouse and left the cottage. The shop was empty when she went in. A young girl, slim, with long dark hair and a small face, came through from the back room and stood behind the till. Not sure how to proceed, Steph stood looking at the shelves. She hadn't come in to buy anything so pulled some bottles of water from the shelf, hoping Bel would appear. As she approached the till, Bel came into the shop with some packs of toilet rolls and, ignoring her, began to pile them up behind the bleach, then came over to the girl.

'Now, sweetheart, how about putting the kettle on and I'll serve this lady.'

'Rick's daughter,' Bel said to Steph coldly. 'She's a sweet girl, and helps me whenever she comes over. Looks like she might be here to stay this time. You're going home tomorrow, I hear. Bet you're glad to be on your way.'

It was said in such a manner that Steph felt she could only agree, then she took her water and left. Was there no end to the surprises Rick could spring upon her?

She'd thought he was just a decent bloke who liked her and wanted to spend time with her. How wrong she had been.

Her heart felt heavy as she packed up the car on Saturday morning. She should be looking forward to going home but she wasn't. She closed the door and got into the car. She sat looking at the cottage and the garden with a mixture of sad and happy memories. Then she turned the key and set the car in motion. She had to put it all behind her.

As soon as she stepped into her flat on Saturday all Steph really wanted to do was throw her case in the bedroom, have a long soak in the bath and go to bed, but there were phone messages for her and a pile of mail to sort through.

Greg came to pick her up at six thirty and looked very dapper in a crisp striped shirt and pressed trousers. He looked every bit the city business-man. She tried to imagine him running down a sand dune and had a silent chuckle. She kissed him briefly on the cheek and then busied herself locking up and finding her jacket.

'You look tired,' he said. 'Was it awful at the cottage?'

She shook her head. It wasn't even worth trying to explain how she felt. But it was good to be with him again and she supposed he was right. Once she got into the swing of it she would enjoy herself. He helped her into his car and she smiled at him, grateful for a man who cared about her and wasn't playing games with her.

She enjoyed the party. All her friends were there and they all wanted to know about her trip and how she had got on. Greg was constantly at her side, getting her drinks, following her around.

It was a beautiful balmy evening and Greta's garden was full of blossom with plenty of seating scattered around, and music filtering out from her conservatory. Steph managed to dodge Greg at one point when he was busy explaining some banking detail to one of their friends, but eventually he tracked her down talking to one of the office crowd at the far end of the lawn.

'Wondered where you'd got to,' he said, taking her arm. She had to bite her tongue not to be rude to him.

When it became chilly they moved inside and Steph relaxed. She'd forgotten how many friends she had here and it was good to see them again. She'd had some wine and was fooling around with Craig from the office doing some strange dance steps he was trying to show her, which had everyone watching them and rolling about in laughter. Greg came up and took her arm to draw her away.

'I think it's time we went home,' he said.

'Not yet,' she replied. 'I'm in the party mood.'

'I'm ready to go,' he said. 'I have a golf tournament in the morning and I need a good night's sleep.'

'You go on ahead, Greg. I can give Steph a lift when she's ready. I go her way,' Craig said.

Greg looked flustered.

'No, I brought her and I'll take her home.'

Steph looked from one to the other.

'You go, Greg. Honestly, I'll be fine,' she said.

Greg grabbed her arm more tightly.

'No, you won't. You are coming with me.'

She couldn't believe he was being so bombastic about it. Everyone was looking shocked. Craig backed off. Greta came to see what the fuss was about.

Greg was looking very red in the face. Steph could feel a nasty situation arising and quickly tried to stop it.

'OK, Greg, let's go,' she said.

When they got in the car she challenged him.

'Why did you do that, making a show of us in front of everyone?'

'You were the one making the show, dancing like that,' he said.

'Dancing like what?' She was incensed. 'I was enjoying myself. That's what parties are for, isn't it?'

He continued to stare at the road ahead.

'I don't like it when you fool around with other men,' he said.

'That's ridiculous. You know all of them. I was just having a lark with Craig. What's got into you?'

'I don't want you carrying on like that. You went to the barbecue with me and I expected you to stay with me instead of going off all evening talking to everyone.'

'So you expected me to stay with you all evening and not talk to anyone else? That's ridiculous.'

'I feel responsible for you. You're my girl. I care about you. Is that a crime?'

'Greg, I am not your girl. I never have been, you know that. We are friends and that is all. I do not expect you to stop me from talking to my friends when we go out. It has to stop. It's not what I want and you know it.'

They'd drawn up outside her flat and he'd opened the door for her to get out.

'It's what I want, Steph. We've had this casual arrangement for too long. I want us to be a proper couple, in a proper relationship.'

She was standing in front of him now. 'Greg, that isn't going to happen. I've always made that clear. Perhaps we should call it a day. I like you very much as a friend, but that is all it can ever be.'

The look of hurt in his eyes gave her great pain. He said nothing but turned, got back in his car and drove off, leaving her standing on the pavement.

She went in to her flat with a heavy heart. What had she done? They'd been friends for many years and shared many good times, and he did care for her — maybe more than anyone else ever would — and she'd thrown it all away.

But there was a sense of relief that it was over. She valued her independence, but would miss not having someone to share a meal with, someone to talk over the day with. The flat seemed empty now and so did she. But it was not Greg she imagined in the empty chair. It was Rick.

On Monday morning her stomach twisted at the thought of the office and what she had to face when she got there. Holidays were all well and good, but there was always the backlog of work that nobody else dealt with and she seemed to have no enthusiasm for it.

The week did not improve as it went along. By Friday she sighed with relief as she left her desk to go home. Somehow the spark had gone out of it. There was something lacking and she couldn't put a finger on it. The job was the same, the people were the same.

But she wasn't the same.

When she got home there was a message on her phone. Mr and Mrs Barnes had agreed to pay the asking price for the cottage and wanted to proceed as quickly as possible.

'We're lucky,' Bradley told her. 'I never expected to get such a good offer so quickly. They loved the garden. I think that's what sold it. You obviously did a good job.'

Steph put down the phone after listening to the message and felt a gut-wrenching twist. She hadn't expected it to happen so soon. Deep down, she had thought the Barnes's would probably reject it after considering all its faults. But they hadn't. They were going to buy it. It wouldn't be her cottage any more.

She knew she had to go back; there were things she hadn't had time to sort out, things she wanted to bring back with her. People she needed to say goodbye to. She had to get the furniture cleared out, lock up for the last time and leave. Despite all the heartache she'd been through, her cottage was still drawing her back. She needed to go back. Maybe she could see him again. She didn't want that terrible meeting to be her lasting memory of them together.

It took all her powers of persuasion to get another week off so soon. Work had been frantic, with important clients to see and pension schemes to set up for a big company she had given a presentation to.

'You know, you're really going places,' Geoff had told her. 'You bring in more business to the company than anyone else in this area. I've put you forward for promotion and you'll be in line for a hefty bonus at the end of the year if you carry on like this. But you must stay focused, Steph. You can't keep taking time off.'

'This will be the last,' she assured him. 'Anyway, I work all the time I'm there. I'm on my laptop every day arranging meetings and answering emails, and I catch up on all my reading. You'll hardly notice I'm not here.'

During the weeks since she'd been back, the cottage had been forced to the back of her mind. But there were times when she would think about Rick and wonder what problems life was throwing at him.

Occasionally she thought about Greg. He hadn't been in contact and she hadn't rung him. What was the point? But she did miss him. Life seemed empty without him coming over in the evenings and sharing a meal with her. She missed the theatre outings and trips to the wine bar, and the meals in expensive restaurants. She even missed him fussing over her in his overbearing way.

The evening before she was leaving for the cottage he appeared on her doorstep looking very sheepish and holding a bottle of her favourite white wine and a large bunch of flowers.

She almost pulled him in she was so pleased to see him.

'I'm sorry,' he said. 'Can we get back to where we were, do you think? I miss you and all the good times we had together.'

She smiled at him.

'I miss you, too, but — '

'I know what all the buts are. You've told me so many times. But our friendship is too valuable to lose.'

They shared the wine and the meal she had cooked for herself, and they talked and talked and the friendship did seem to be back on track. He left about ten and she went to bed feeling content.

'At least you're only going to be away for the week this time,' Greg said when he phoned her the next morning. 'In fact, if it hadn't been for the golf club championship matches on Saturday, I could have come with you. Couldn't you put it off till next week?'

She could have done but something stopped her. She wanted to be alone. There was still one cupboard to sort, the one she had been putting off, the one with all the old boxes in. She had been tempted to just dump them, but it didn't seem right to do that. There might be something of importance amongst the nostalgia. But she knew it would be a heart-wrenching job and she wanted to do it alone.

'I'm only going up there to do a last sort out and make sure everything is ready to hand over. The sale is progressing without problems. It should be completed very soon. Then it will be done with,' she told him.

'I'm glad to hear it.' And he left her in peace.

So here she was again on the motorway and heading for Southport. It was late on Friday when she arrived. Struggling to get her key in the lock, she noticed the ivy covering the front had been trimmed back, and when she turned and squinted in the moonlight, she saw that the front hedge had been cut and the grass mown. Jim had been here; he'd said he'd keep an eye on it for her. He was such a kind man. She would go and see them first thing in the morning.

It felt warm and cosy inside after the

chill of the evening and it was peaceful after all the hustle and bustle of London. Life here was lived at a different pace altogether and she tried to imagine what it would be like to come home to this at the end of each day instead of her flat. Then her eyes began to feel very heavy and she took herself off to bed.

When she woke she was amazed to find it was nine o'clock. It was too much trouble to run a bath so she slid into her jeans and decided to have a soak later in the day, when she had at least accomplished something of what she had come here to do.

Jim and Elsie were delighted to see her and made her sit and have a cup of tea with them.

'I really just came to see how you were coping with your ankle and to apologise for not being in touch. Work has been impossible and I've had a lot on after work, too.'

'Aye, it were fine in no time with your bandaging,' Elsie said.

'Sounds like you need this break, lass,' Jim said. 'You want to take it easy and not go mad trying to make it spick and span.'

'I've got to sort out some stuff in the big cupboard this weekend. I was so busy trying to get it presentable for sale that I put off sorting the personal stuff. I expect it will all go in the bin. Then when everything is signed and sealed I'll get a removal firm to take the furniture away.'

'Aren't you going to keep some of it?' Elsie asked. 'But I suppose you've got everything you want. You young people these days have it all.'

'I will take something, as you say, and if there's anything you want then you can help yourself. You've been so good to me. Oh, and thank you for doing the ivy and the hedge. It makes the place look much more cared for.'

'Aye. lass, I didn't do ought. It were young Rick who did that. He's been there at the cottage near every day. He seems to have taken you under his wing. I think he enjoys the peace and quiet. He's got more than his fair share of trouble there, I can tell you.' He chuckled until Elsie shushed him.

'I thought he was staying with his father. Sally told me Fiona was back at the house.'

'She is, and she's staying put this time it seems. I don't know where Rick's living, but he's still working there. They couldn't run that place without him.'

Steph had made up her mind not to enter into any further discussions about Rick and had tried desperately to put him out of her mind, but this news disturbed her. It shouldn't matter to her where he was living or working, or whether Fiona was staying or going. But it did. She wished he wouldn't keep doing her garden. Yet part of her desperately wanted to see him again.

It was afternoon before she opened the big white cupboard at the side of the fireplace and stood on a stool to reach the top shelf where the boxes were. There were three, two of them cardboard shoe boxes and one big wooden box which was locked. First she tackled the shoe boxes, hoping that they might yield the key to the wooden box, as it hadn't turned up anywhere else in the cottage.

There were a few sepia photos of people she didn't know, and some birthday cards from various members of the family. There was a newspaper cutting of when Steph had gone to university and another of her engagement to Simon. It was days now since she'd thought about Simon and she'd begun to think she was finally over him, though she knew she would never trust a man again.

Then there were newspaper clippings of various important events, and a big one of her aunt winning a prize at the Southport Flower Show for her roses. She put aside a few to keep, but most of it meant little to her.

After emptying both shoe boxes, the key to the wooden box still hadn't turned up. It must hold something of importance and Steph felt quite nervous holding it. She remembered a jewellery box in a drawer in Rose's bedroom with all sorts of bits and pieces in it. Maybe the key would be amongst that lot. She darted up the stairs and opened the drawer. There was a tiny key there in the box. She rushed back downstairs and tried it in the lock. It fitted exactly.

There was movement outside the front window and Steph saw that Bel was pushing open the gate. Her heart sank. The last thing she wanted now was a confrontation. But she couldn't pretend she wasn't in. The window was wide open and her car was parked on the gravel. She opened the door and Bel looked at her uncomfortably.

'May I come in?' she asked.

Steph stood aside to let her in and they went into the front room.

'Sorry about all the mess,' Steph apologised. 'I'm just having a last sort out.'

'So, you've sold it, have you?'

'Looks like it. I'm waiting for the final papers then I'll be off.' This was probably what Bel wanted to hear. It should clear the air.

But Bel looked so downcast she wondered what the problem was. Steph moved some bin liners off the sofa.

'Come and sit down.'

But Bel stood by the door, reluctant to come in any further. Then she seemed to gather courage and said it all in a rush.

'Look, I'm sorry for being the way I was. You didn't deserve it. It was just me. I get like that sometimes when I'm upset. I don't seem to be able to handle it.'

Steph nodded.

'It's OK. I understand. I'm sorry, too. I didn't know the situation.'

Bel relaxed and sighed.

'I'm afraid there isn't any situation, except in my head.'

'I know exactly what you mean. He took me in, too,' Steph said.

Bel shook her head.

'No, you've got that wrong.'

'What do you mean?'

Bel looked wretched.

'Rick is really taken with you. I've always liked him, stupid old fool that I am. But I knew in my heart he didn't feel the same. But he's such a lovely man and I hate to see him unhappy.'

'What are you saying?' Steph said.

'Rick's never stopped talking about you since you went away. He's driving us all crazy asking if we've seen you or if you're coming back. He's at your cottage every day.'

Steph could feel her legs going weak.

'I didn't think he cared about me at all. Sometimes he wouldn't be in touch for days, then turn up as if nothing was wrong. And he never told me about Fiona. She seems to still have a hold over him.'

Bel looked deflated.

'Look, let me make us a cup of tea and we can have a proper talk. I'm just glad you came round. I didn't want to go away leaving it the way it was. Not after you'd been so kind to me when I arrived.'

Bel smiled and looked a little more relaxed.

'Thanks, Steph. You've no idea how much courage it took me to come. I thought you'd bite my head off.'

Steph was taken aback.

'Did you really?'

Bel shrugged and looked a little sheepish.

'You do seem a little intimidating. Even Sally said she wouldn't like to get on the wrong side of you.'

'Oh, dear,' Steph said. As she waited for the kettle to boil she wondered how many other people felt that way about her. Maybe Rick did.

Bel perched on the edge of the sofa and Steph cleared one of the chairs of papers and sat opposite to her.

'So what's all this about Rick? I really think you've got it all wrong. Why would he have behaved the way he did if he'd cared?'

'Because Fiona's back, that's why.'

'I thought they were divorced. Sally said she was his ex-wife.'

'Didn't he tell you about his plans?'

'No, he didn't.' Steph had the feeling she wasn't going to like what she was about to hear.

Bel looked down at her tea.

'Maybe it's not my place to tell you, then.'

Steph was getting annoyed. Why did everyone hint about it but never let her into the mystery? Even Rick had been evasive.

'OK, then don't tell me. I don't know why it matters. So long as she keeps out of my way it's not my problem.'

Bel became flustered.

'Oh, Steph, don't let's fall out again. I will tell you. I think you have a right to know.'

Steph sat still and drank her tea. She wasn't sure she wanted to know anymore. She and Bel had made their peace and the cottage was sold. She needed to get all this stuff sorted and then get back home.

'Fiona wants to live at Boland's again,' Bel said.

'I gathered that, but what's it got to do with me?'

'It's got a lot to do with you,' Bel said.

'You're not making any sense.' She could only control the hurt inside her by being angry. She certainly wasn't going to cry in front of Bel.

Bel carried on talking.

'Fiona wants Rick to carry on working and living there. He can't be expected to do that. Not after what's happened. I really hope she doesn't talk him into it. He might give it a go for Bryony's sake, but it would never work.'

'But what's the alternative if Fiona decides to stay?'

'He's talking about getting a job somewhere away from here. It's only to get away from her. He shouldn't be forced to leave his own village because she decides to come back. But Rick's like that. He'll do anything for a peaceful life. Either way it's not right. He's in an impossible position.'

'I agree. But I suppose he's the only one who can decide what's best. I still don't see what it has to do with me.'

'I think you could stop him if you wanted to. He really does seem to be smitten with you.'

She felt the panic rising. She had to keep control. She wasn't going to let Bel see how she felt. She doubted very much whether she could influence Rick and why would she want to? Her life wasn't here, so what would be the point?

'Bel, look, can we leave it. I really don't think I can help Rick and I do have a lot of clearing out to do.'

Bel stopped and looked uncomfortable.

'I wanted you to know that if you and Rick did get together I'd be happy for you. He deserves better than he's got and he's mad about you, whatever you say. It would affect his decision if he thought you cared about him.'

Steph shook her head.

'Bel, I've sold the cottage and I'm going back to London. Rick will sort out his own life. He has a lot to consider and it's not my place to interfere.'

Bel shifted uneasily on the sofa then stood up.

'Sorry, Steph, I should mind my own business.'

Bel was by the door now, and Steph winced at the droop of her shoulders.

'Bel, don't go like this.'

Bel turned, a look of resignation on her face. Steph was trying hard to hold it all together.

'I'm glad you came. And thank you for being so honest with me. I care about Rick, just as you do.' She smiled weakly. 'We're both in the same boat.'

Bel tried but couldn't manage a smile.

'No, not really. He loves you.'

When Bel had gone Steph was so confused she couldn't think straight. She felt for Bel, knew the pain she was suffering and yet somewhere inside her sprung a seed of hope. Rick loved her. That's what Bel had said.

After staring at the box for several minutes she finally turned the key, then hesitated before opening the lid, wondering what she was about to find. Why had this box been locked? Maybe she shouldn't open it. Yet she couldn't dump it without finding out what was in it. Rose must have known she would find it.

She cautiously lifted the lid, almost afraid of what she might find inside. After only a few minutes her heart started pounding. What she was discovering inside was a complete shock. Tied in delicate pink ribbon was a bundle of letters that were obviously very personal. With shaking hands she undid the ribbon then hesitated. Was she intruding into something she had no business with? But she couldn't stop. She needed to know. It was important.

As she read the first letter her eyes were beginning to fill with tears. They were love letters. From someone who signed himself 'A'. It seemed they'd been communicating when Rose must have been about her age, and the friendship had become progressively more loving. He told her how she made his life bearable and how he wished they could be together. It seemed he took her to concerts and occasionally out for a meal. But there was never a mention of commitment.

Then the letters had become sad and pleading. Her aunt had obviously decided to stop all contact. It seemed as if things had been getting out of hand and she felt it was dangerous and many people were going to get hurt. 'A' was distraught.

Steph sat there for over an hour glued to the letters. They were dated and kept in order so they read like a book. As she read the last one she felt her throat tighten and she carefully folded it and placed it back with the others.

She needed to get away from the cottage; a blow along the seafront at

Southport was what she wanted. She always felt better when she was near the sea. It was in her blood and she found it soothing. She didn't bother to change, just jumped in the car and drove, her mind turning over and over, wondering who this mystery man could be and whether it was anyone she had known. Was he still alive? Dare she ask Elsie? Her head was bursting with questions.

She parked the car and started at a brisk pace along towards Rotten Row, a place she'd always loved. She wanted the comfort of returning to a time when she was happy, when worries were unknown and heartache something she had never experienced. She'd walk through the park and then make her way down on to the beach.

She sat on a bench in the park and watched a mum sitting on the grass playing with a toddler. That was something she would never do. She got up and walked again. She was lonely. She needed to talk to someone. Her heart was bursting with love and pain and sadness.

Then she remembered she had never picked up the desk Rick's father had said she could have. She'd been so busy it had completely gone out of her mind and Rick had obviously forgotten it, too. She'd call on him and ask if she could pick up the desk on her way home.

He answered immediately when she pressed his number and sounded delighted she'd come, so she made her way up to his flat.

'Come in, dear,' he said. 'What a pleasure to see you.'

'I hope I'm not disturbing you,' she said. 'I just wondered if I could pick up the desk.'

'Now, why has that lad of mine not been for it? It's much too heavy for you to manage on your own. I suppose he's busy with his greenhouses at this time of year, and all sorts of other problems, from what I hear. Maybe I can help you with it. Now, tell me, how are you progressing with the cottage? My son is still helping you, I hope.'

'Yes, he's been very kind. He's done a

lot in the garden whilst I've been away. It looks lovely.'

'And now you're back again, I see. Are you staying long this time?'

'No, I just have to sort out the furniture before the sale goes through.'

'Well, you sit there and I'll put the kettle on. You're not going to dash off this time, I hope.'

'A cup of tea would be lovely.' She was already feeling much calmer.

They chatted amiably for a while. He wanted to know all about the cottage and seemed very interested in her progress in sorting it.

'I've been sorting boxes of personal stuff today,' she told him and he gave her a wry smile.

'Always a distressing business. But it has to be done.'

She was tempted to tell him what she had found. It would have been a relief to share it with someone who didn't know her aunt and wouldn't gossip or be judgemental. He seemed to be waiting for her to continue, but she couldn't do it. It would have been disloyal to Rose to tell anyone what she had found. Then the moment had passed.

'When are your buyers hoping to complete?' he asked.

'Very soon, I hope.'

'You'll be glad to be finished with it. I expect. It must be difficult finding the time in your busy life to worry about a little cottage in the back of beyond.'

'Yes, I will be relieved when it's settled.'

'Do I detect a little reluctance there?' His eyes were so like Rick's and she had to look away.

'It's the end of my family ties, I suppose. Always a bit of a wrench. I was very fond of my aunt.'

He was looking at her again in that way, but all he said was, 'Yes.'

They drank their tea and talked easily until she felt much more like herself. Then she went to get her car and they managed to get the desk down and into it.

'Thank you for letting me have it. It

means a lot to me.'

'You're welcome. I'm glad it's found a good home.'

When she got it back to the cottage she was tempted to leave it in the car. It wouldn't fit in with the decor in her flat and she couldn't help wondering what Greg would think of it. He hated clutter.

She looked at it as it lay on its side in the back of her car and couldn't resist trying to get it out. She wanted it in the cottage, even if only for a few days. So she struggled and as her frustration grew so did her strength, and at last she managed to slide it on to the ground. It was solid oak and enormously heavy, but eventually she edged it into the hall and into the front room.

She stood back and looked at it. There was an inkwell and some carved initials on the lid. She lifted the lid. That was heavy, too, and she remembered hiding behind it one day when she hadn't learned her seven times tables and had hoped she wouldn't be picked on to answer. It hadn't worked, just drawn attention to her.

Inside was a large stiff envelope, the sort used to hold a certificate. She looked inside to see if it contained anything of importance that she should return. There was a photograph of men dressed in suits at some sort of a function, and in the front row was Rick's father, a lot younger but still recognisable. The envelope was addressed to a *Mr Austin Jameson* at the address she had just been to. Her heart missed a beat. This was the 'A' in the letters. Everything hit her in a flash. It all fitted. The way he'd said yes when she'd said how fond she was of her aunt, the pause for her to continue when she'd mentioned the box, the look he'd given her when she'd told him she'd been sorting personal stuff.

She collapsed into the chair, gripping the photo in her hand. Austin Jameson, Rick's father. She knew it. She'd seen that look in his eyes before when she'd mentioned her aunt, but hadn't been able to interpret it until now. Suddenly it all made sense. He hadn't known whether she had found out his secret or not and hadn't known whether to confide in her. How sad he must be feeling now she had died and the cottage was to go.

A million things were milling round in her head. She had to see him. She had to take the photo back. She couldn't leave him wondering how many people knew his secret.

When Samantha phoned from the office, asking her for some information she needed for one of their clients, she had to shake herself back into reality.

'Are you with me, Steph? You sound a bit vague. I sent you an e-mail about it yesterday. I promised to get back to him today.'

'Yes, sorry. I'll e-mail it to you straight away. Been a bit busy with one thing and another.'

Samantha seemed pacified, but Steph knew she should have acted more promptly. Geoff had only let her come away again so soon on condition she kept in touch and continued to work.

It was just that everything here seemed so much more important and real. She was beginning to feel at home in this cottage, and the people here were becoming friends. Now this new discovery made it even more difficult to detach herself from it.

She shook herself and got up and poured a glass of wine. What was she thinking? Her life and her work were miles away in London. She was doing well, in line for promotion and well thought of by the company she worked for. She had a good social life, a smart flat, and Greg. What more could she want? Certainly not a tumbledown cottage in this tiny village and getting involved with a man with a past. And a present, as she now realised.

The phone rang again and she knew it would be Greg.

'Hi, how's it going?' He seemed happy again and she hoped they could sustain their friendship on that basis for a long time, as she valued his support and reliability.

'Fine. Everything is sorted now. I just need to tie up last-minute bits with the solicitor then I'll be home.'

'Can't you do that by phone?' There was an edge to his voice again.

'Yes, I could, but I prefer to do it in person in his office. Saves sending everything through the post.'

When she'd put the phone down she knew she had been making excuses. What she'd meant was that it gave her an extra few days to relax in her cottage, and to be near Rick.

She could not stop herself thinking about what Bel had said. Did he really care about her that much? Did he love her? Could she really stop him going away? That lump came in her throat again and she swallowed. She couldn't let her thoughts run along those lines. He needed to get away, start the life he wanted, in a job he wanted. He had the opportunity to break free and do something that had always been denied him.

She realised she was still clutching

the photo. Staring at it again, she saw how like Rick his father was. It must have been taken some time ago. She made a decision. Tomorrow when she went into Southport to the solicitor she would take the photo back and tell him about the letters.

Saying Goodbye

Before she went to see Austin she decided to pay Rick a visit and thank him for looking after the garden while she was away. She wanted to see him one last time and put things right between them. Then she could go home and forget about the cottage and everything else here.

With some trepidation she walked down the path and round to the back of the house to the barn. He had his office there and had told her he was usually there in the afternoons.

He wasn't in the barn or in his office. There was a large glass lean-to at the back of the house and the door was open. She knocked on the glass but nothing happened. Wondering if she should go in she gave one more rather loud knock on the glass. The young girl she'd seen in Bel's shop came sauntering through in shorts and bare feet — Rick's daughter. She looked to be in her early teens and had a precocious air about her.

'Hello,' Steph said.

The girl didn't reply, just stood there staring at her.

'Is your father in? Could I have a word with him?' Steph was trying to keep the tremor out of her voice.

The girl shrugged.

'Don't know if he's about. Hang on, I'll call him. He might be in the shed.' With that she pushed past Steph and yelled out, 'Dad, there's someone to see you.' Then she disappeared back into the house.

He came ambling round the hedge in old trousers and up to his elbows in soil. But his smile was the same.

'Well, this is a surprise,' he said.

She was melting in those eyes. This was the worst moment she could remember, but she had to do it and not break down.

'I just came to say goodbye and to thank you for everything. You've helped me a lot and we had some good times together. I'd like to remember them rather than the angry exchange we had before I left last time.'

He shook his head and the smile slowly melted away but he didn't speak. He came towards her and the look in his eyes as he held hers was difficult to bear, but she couldn't look away.

'Steph, why do you have to go?'

'Because I don't belong here,' she replied.

He looked distraught and she was afraid they would both break down.

'Look, can we go inside?' he asked.

She followed him into a large kitchen with a table in the centre and a cooking range taking up half of one wall. The stone floor sent up a chill and she shivered. There was no sign of the girl, but she could hear noisy music coming from somewhere inside. And there was no sign of Fiona, for which she was very grateful.

'Sorry about the noise.' He smiled. 'Bryony's the same as all teenagers, I'm afraid. Sit down, please,' he said.

She perched on one of the chairs at the table and he pulled out the one opposite.

'Steph, I'm sorry about all this. It's a mess. I didn't mean to deceive you. I didn't know she was coming back. We've been divorced for over a year.'

'Look, Rick, this has nothing to do with me. I wish you'd put me in the picture from the beginning, but it doesn't matter now. I've sold the cottage and I'm going home. I didn't want to go without thanking you. I could never have done it without your help. The garden sold the cottage, I'm sure of it.'

He looked so weary her heart went out to him. It was time to leave. She'd done what she came for. He watched her get up and didn't argue, seeming almost too weary to put up any more resistance.

'I've enjoyed it, too. I just wish you weren't going. But I can see you've made up your mind so I have to accept it.'

He continued to sit at the table and

watched her leave without another word.

Her heart was heavy as she walked the short distance back to the cottage. As she opened the door the phone was ringing and she just got to it in time.

'Steph, it's Bradley. I'm afraid I have some bad news for you. Your buyers have pulled out.'

'What? Can they do that at this late stage? I thought they were really keen on getting the cottage.'

'They were, but unfortunately Mr Barnes has had a stroke and is in hospital.'

'Oh, how dreadful. Was it a bad one?' She felt genuine compassion for the couple. They were nice people.

'He's evidently off the danger list and expected to make a recovery of sorts. But they realise that there is no way now that they can move in the foreseeable future and that he won't ever be fit enough to carry out the restoration of the cottage he had planned.'

'I see. Yes, I can understand that. Couldn't we give them a little more time?' She was as much concerned about the Barneses as of losing the sale of the cottage.

'I'm afraid they are adamant about it. Mrs Barnes just wants her husband to come home and recover in peace.'

'Of course. So where do we stand now? Do you have anyone else interested?'

'I'm afraid not. We were very lucky to get any interest at all. They were a gift from heaven; Mr Barnes being a builder and able to do the place up himself. There aren't many like him around who would want to take on a place like yours. But we'll keep on trying. Never give up hope is what I say.'

Hope. What hope did she have of selling her cottage? What hope did she have of finding love? What hope did she have of a happy and fulfilled life? She put her head in her hands and wept. It was self indulgent, she knew, and something she rarely allowed herself to do, but today she felt justified.

Now she had to go back home and play the waiting game, until at some point the whole place would fall down in a tangle of weeds and rubble and someone would cart it all away and build something grotesque in its place.

The afternoon stretched before her with little to do. What was the point in gardening, when in a few weeks it would be a wilderness again? She couldn't keep taking time off to come here. Geoff had been understanding, but there was a limit and she knew she was at it. The only thing she had to do now, before packing up the car with things she wanted to take home, was to return the photo.

Rick's father was pleased to see her and to have his photo returned.

'Do call me Austin, my dear. We can't always be this formal. I feel we are friends already.'

She smiled uncomfortably. He didn't realise how apt that was.

'I don't know how it got there,' he continued, looking at the photo. 'I was sure I emptied it the other day knowing you were going to pick it up. I'm sorry you've had the trouble of bringing it back. But it is really nice to see you.'

He made tea and brought two mugs back into the living-room where she was sitting.

'I remember that being taken. It was a Pharmaceutical Society dinner. We always dressed to the nines in those days. All very formal.' He studied the photo. 'I always thought Rick would follow in my footsteps and take over the shop, but he always wanted to be a gardener. Went to college, got all the qualifications, then ended up working in that place. I wish he could disentangle himself from it and move on. I would love to see him happy.'

'It's a shame. He loves gardening so much and he's so good at it. He's turned the cottage garden into a little haven. I love it. And so did Mrs Barnes.' She told him how they had had to back out of the sale and how sorry she was to hear of their bad luck. She wasn't going to mention what Bel had told her about Rick's plans. That was up to Rick to tell his father himself.

He shook his head.

'That is sad. I'm very sorry to hear it. Now you have to start all over again. At least you have the garden under control. Someone else will fall in love with it, I'm sure.'

'I think Rick could easily get a job landscaping gardens. He's wasting his talent at Boland's, and if he dislikes it so much he's wasting his life as well,' she said.

Austin's face twisted with anger.

'It was that wife of his. She talked him into marrying her. I told him not to, that it would all end in tears, but he wouldn't listen. Headstrong, that lad. Just like his mother. Then she insisted on him working there. Her father owned it, you see. I think Rick liked the old man so was happy to oblige, but once the old fella died the trouble started.'

Austin was on a roll and Steph didn't interrupt. He was pacing the room, becoming more agitated, turning frequently to face her, his face showing the anger he felt.

'She inherited the lot. She never let Rick forget she owned the place and that she was boss. He wanted to make changes that would have made the business more viable, but she would have none of it. Next thing she's up and off with her fancy man.'

He paused and looked at Steph.

'I'm sorry, my dear. I'm behaving very badly. You don't want to hear all this.'

His face had settled itself into its usual composure, but she could see he was still upset. She got up from the chair and went to him, touching his shoulder gently and he tried to smile.

'I'm sorry,' she said. 'I can understand how you feel. It does seem Rick has been treated very badly.'

He shook his head and walked across to the window to look out over the leafy road, then he turned towards her.

'Rick's got the place back on its feet since he's been left to it. It's a good business. But now she's back I don't know what will happen. Rick's still running it, but he can't carry on with that woman on his back all the time.'

'He should leave her to it,' Steph said.

'Of course he should. But Rick's not like that. Too kind and easy going for his own good. And he's always thinking about Bryony. That's why he stayed on and kept it going.'

Steph was thoughtful.

'I suppose that's why he's let her move back in and he's moved out. So Bryony can have her home back.'

'Bryony's his main concern, certainly. She's never been happy since they moved out, never wanted to leave the village and her friends. Fiona wouldn't let her visit regularly. I think she was afraid she'd make a fuss and want to stay.'

He looked apologetic.

'I'm sorry. I shouldn't be unburdening myself to you. You have your own problems. Why on earth did she have to come back now, just when he was beginning to look like his old self again?

He enjoyed working on your garden and he seemed very fond of you. I can see why.' He gave her a wry smile.

The photograph had fallen to the floor and he bent to pick it up and straighten it out. When he looked up he seemed to have recovered his composure.

'Now, tell me your plans.' Then that look appeared in his eyes again as he studied her face. 'Is it what you want, my dear?'

'What do you mean?' She was forced to hold his look.

'I mean, do you really want to sell the cottage and move back to your London life?'

She was stunned.

'Why do you ask?'

He smiled.

'I have a feeling you rather like it here. You seem a lot happier and more relaxed than when you first came down to see it. Are you sure this way of life isn't getting into your bones? You're a Southport girl, as I remember. You can't deny your birthright.'

She sighed.

'You have a point. I often wish I could just curl up on that old chair in the cottage and never have to worry about work and London life ever again. But I have to earn a living, and that's in the city.'

'Of course, you must ignore the ramblings of an elderly man. I hope all goes well. Some day, someone will fall in love with it as you have done.'

She left thinking about what he had said. Had she fallen in love with the cottage? Was it still just a cottage or was it *her* cottage?

She hadn't managed to broach the subject of the letters, and she still didn't know what to do with them.

Half an hour after she got home Rick appeared, and she couldn't help a spark of joy at seeing him standing there.

'May I come in and explain? I really don't want you going away thinking badly of me.'

After hearing what Austin had said,

she felt much more sympathetic towards him, had a greater understanding of his situation.

'Of course. I felt bad when I left you. You seemed so down, but I didn't see how I could help.'

He followed her into the kitchen and stood behind her as they looked out over the garden. As she turned, his eyes held hers and she wanted to hug him and try to make it all better. But she was out of her depth when it came to family disputes. He had an ex-wife, a daughter and a whole business to contend with. What would he want with her at a time like this?

He seemed in no hurry to explain whatever it was he'd come for and continued to look out of the window.

'We did a good job on the garden, didn't we?'

'Yes, it's a lovely peaceful place now.'

Again there was a long silence, then he faced her again, his mouth contorted with emotion.

'Steph, why do you have to sell the

cottage? Why don't you come and live here? You know you want to.'

'What do you mean?' She moved away from him. 'I have a life in London. It's where I live and where I work.'

'But it doesn't have to be. Maybe this was the chance you needed to start a new life.'

'I don't want to start a new life. I've worked hard to get where I am. I'm not about to throw it all away on a whim.'

'I think you're making a big mistake,' Rick said. 'The cottage falling through seems like an omen to me. It's giving you a second chance to consider. Just tell me you'll think about it.'

She stood looking at him and her heart was heavy.

'But you have your own life to sort out. You have a business and a daughter and Fiona. Why are you concerned about what I do?'

He shrugged and gave her a wan smile.

'I thought that would have been very obvious.' He took her hand. 'Come into the garden with me. I want to show you something.'

She let him lead her out of the kitchen and over the grass. He stopped by the pond and bent to smooth the grass away from a moss-covered stone. She saw that the moss had been scraped away from part of it and that there was writing engraved on the stone.

He looked up at her.

'Come and look at it,' he said very softly. She bent beside him and tried to make out the faint words. *Follow Your Dream*, it said. 'I found it when I was clearing out the pond.'

Steph gazed at the words then looked up at Rick.

'Aunt Rose didn't follow her dream.'

'No, she didn't.'

'She did what she knew was right.'

He shook his head.

'No, I think she got it wrong.'

So he knew about Rose and Austin. He knew and he'd never said.

'How did you feel about what

happened?' she asked.

He stood up.

'I didn't think much at the time. I was only a child. But later I heard the rumours, and one day I asked Dad whether they were true. He told me they were. I didn't blame him.'

'Didn't you feel he'd betrayed your mother?' They were standing very close by the pond, facing each other.

'Yes, I did at first. But the more I thought about it, the more I could see it his way. Mother was a remote person. I never had a good relationship with her. I always felt I was in the way; that I'd spoilt her life somehow. It was Dad I always related to.'

'Do you think they were happy?'

'I think they jogged along together. They didn't row. Dad doesn't like unpleasantness. He'll do a lot to avoid it.'

'You mean the way you did with Fiona?'

'Yes, I tried to please her. But in the end it wasn't enough. Life wasn't exciting enough for her. So she left me. Steve offered her the Earth. He had money then, a place in Spain, a boat.'

'So why's she back?'

'Oh, his business isn't doing so well. They've been rowing a lot. She says it's upsetting Bryony.'

'And does she want to get back with you?'

'Yes.' He said it without emotion, his eyes never leaving hers.

'Is that what you want?' She could feel the tremble in her legs and her hands wouldn't stay still. It was what she had feared, yet had not acknowledged. This one word seemed to shatter her world.

Then he took her in his arms and held her very close. She dislodged herself with a will power she didn't know she had, and just about managed to say, 'I have to get on.' She turned and walked back into the house, leaving him looking after her, motionless.

When he came into the kitchen she was busying herself making tea and she didn't look at him until he came close and stopped her by putting his hand over hers.

'Steph, I didn't say I was willing to do that.'

She managed to look at him.

'You have to give it a go, for Bryony's sake.'

'I don't have to.'

She looked away, couldn't stand firm with that look he was giving her.

'Yes, Rick, you do. We both have commitments. We don't have the freedom to follow our dreams.'

'Steph, look at me, please.'

She did and it took all the strength she could muster.

'Is that what you really want?' he asked.

She held his gaze.

'Yes, Rick, it's what I want.'

He nodded, then slowly turned and walked away. She was left staring out of the window towards the pond, her heart breaking.

It was with a heavy heart that Rick

strode down the lane in the direction of Boland's. He didn't want to go back there, didn't want to face all the discussions and questions. He hadn't wanted to leave Steph the way things were between them. Yet what right did he have to try to persuade her to give up her career and stay in the cottage?

He had never felt like this about any woman before. He loved her and he cared about her. He wanted her to stay and be with him. It was a selfish desire on his part to keep her there. He wanted to be able to visualise her in the cottage, in the garden, safe from the stresses of her life in London and safe from Greg.

More than anything he wanted her to be happy, but he couldn't offer her happiness. His life was a mess. If he stayed at Boland's and tried to work with Fiona his life would be hell. If he left he would have to find work elsewhere, maybe a long way from here. Either way he couldn't drag Steph through all that. He had to let her go.

Without thinking, he found his steps taking him to the one place he could find some solace. He had a lot of thinking to do and the marsh was the only place he had ever felt at peace at times like this.

He strode along the spongy wet grass until he came to the hump of dry turf where he always sat with its view out over the open sea to the horizon. Today his head hung low as he stared at the ground. He had no idea where to go from here. Every option he had considered seemed doomed. The only thing he was sure of was that he loved Steph and that he couldn't have her.

Rick Makes His Decision

By Sunday Steph had cleaned the whole place from top to bottom, weeded the garden and cut the grass. The windows were sparkling and she'd even found some brass polish and cleaned all the brass. It looked more homely and she felt better. The hard work had been therapeutic.

Now she was ready for a change and decided she'd go shopping in Southport — anything to keep her mind off Rick. She'd buy some new cushions to replace the tatty ones, some brighter curtains and maybe even some fresh bedding to cheer up the bedroom. That should help sell it.

She was standing beside the toaster waiting for her piece of toast to pop, when a movement in the garden caught her eye. It was Rick pushing a wheel-barrow with a spade in it.

She opened the window and shouted to him.

'What are you doing? I thought you'd finished here.'

He turned and shrugged.

'Thought I should keep it tidy for as long as I can.'

He looked defeated and she wanted to run to him and tell him how she felt, but instead stood at the open window watching him take the spade out of the barrow and throw it on the ground.

'Steph, you know I like coming here because I love this cottage and garden, and it gives me a break.' He looked away into the distance over the hedge. His voice was very low now. 'It makes me feel close to you, even when you're not here.' Then he walked away from the window and continued down the garden.

Why did life have to be so complicated? He had responsibilities and big decisions to make, and she had a job in London. There could be no future for them. There were too many obstacles in the way.

She left the toast in the toaster and Rick in the garden and went off to do her shopping. She had to keep some sort of order in her life and not let events beyond her control toss and turn her in all directions. It was her cottage, her decision what she did with it and how long she stayed in it. If Rick was determined to work in the garden and it gave him some pleasure, then she would let him.

She found some nice cushions and material to make up curtains and hoped she could cope with the old Singer sewing-machine she'd found stored away in a cupboard. It still looked in good condition. It would be fun to see if all the sewing lessons at school all those years ago had produced any results.

She was just coming out of the store when someone tapped her on the shoulder. It was Austin. He looked pleased to see her and she felt a warm glow inside at the sight of him.

'What a coincidence. Of all the

people in town today, fancy bumping into you! I'm very glad I have, mind you.'

He looked very dapper in his smart trousers and jacket. He really was a handsome man for his age, and she loved his old world courtesy.

'You look laden. Can I give you a hand with those parcels?'

'I'm fine, Austin, honestly. But could we have a cuppa somewhere, if you've got time. I'm gasping for one and it would be lovely to have a chat.'

'Of course, my dear, I have all the time in the world. Now, where would you like to go? I suggest the Grosvenor. They do an acceptable afternoon tea and have comfortable chairs. Would that suit?'

'That sounds wonderful. I used to go there with my mum sometimes. She liked it, too. But I wouldn't have gone there on my own. It's much too grand.'

'Then let an old man escort you. It will be my pleasure.'

It was just what she wanted; a comfy

settee in a lovely old hotel and Austin for company. He was so easy to talk to and it made her feel nearer to Rick. Immediately she felt more relaxed and happy.

A waitress dressed smartly in black and white served them with tea and cakes in lovely china cups on a crisp white table cloth.

'Now, tell me what you've been up to. I thought you'd have been back in London by now.'

'I should be.' She hesitated.

'You've fallen in love with that cottage, I can tell.' He smiled.

'Yes, I think I have. I don't know what to do.'

'Well, now, my dear, you must follow your heart.'

A sadness came over him. She wanted so much to say she understood, that she'd seen the letters; that her aunt had kept them safe all those years. He held her with his eyes.

'You know, don't you? You know about Rose and me.'

There was no point in denying it.

'Yes, I'm sorry. I found your letters. She had them locked in a big wooden box. I shouldn't have opened it.'

'No, Steph. I think your aunt wanted you to. I'm glad you did. What did you think when you read them?'

'I didn't connect them with you at first. Not until I found the envelope with your name on.'

'Yes, I thought that might be the case. But what do you think about me now you know?'

'I think you are a lovely, kind man and that you must have had your reasons.'

'I did wrong, Steph. I betrayed my wife. I loved another woman. I'm not proud of what I did. Can I try to explain? It would mean a lot to me. I've never told a soul before.'

'You don't have to. I won't think any the less of you. We all have our reasons for doing things we shouldn't.'

'And are you about to do something you shouldn't?'

'I don't know. I don't think I have a choice.'

'We all have choices. Rose made her choice. I respected it. But I have always wished it could have been different.'

'How did it happen?' She wanted to know and felt he needed to tell her.

'I married Rick's mother after a whirl-wind romance. Monica was beautiful and we were both young. She swept me off my feet. We were happy for a while, then when Rick was born, and she had to give up her work and become a full-time housewife, things started going wrong. She was irritable and hated being at home. Money was tight, too.

'My chemist shop was in the village then. Rose was one of my customers. When she was ill once I took her medicine round to the cottage and that was when it started. I used to go and see her occasionally before returning home in the evening. It became a habit. When the shop closed down I missed her and that was when the letters started, and we'd meet when we could.'

'Why did you stop?' Steph asked.

'Rose was never comfortable with it. I know she loved me, but I was married and she knew I wouldn't leave Monica. I had to think of Rick as well.'

'It must have hurt a lot. How did you cope?' She was thinking of her own situation now.

'Well, after wallowing in self pity for a while, I just gritted my teeth and got on with it. Rose was right. We couldn't have continued the way things were. I couldn't have expected Rose to take second place. Not that she ever did, but it must have seemed so to her.'

'I see.'

He leaned over and took her hand.

'Steph, don't let that happen to you. When you fall in love, grab it in both hands. It's a precious thing. We were never truly happy, Monica and me. We would both have been happier apart. But we had Rick to consider. But you are young and have no ties. Don't let love slip by.'

'But I'm not in love.' She was trying

to convince herself. 'I was once, but he left me. It broke my heart at the time. I don't want to go through that again.'

'Oh, dear, now I've upset you. That's the last thing you need when you have so much on your plate.'

He had been so honest with her that she wondered if she could broach the subject of Rick.

'Rick's in the same boat, isn't he? I suppose he has to think about Bryony.'

'It's a terrible business. I don't know what he's going to do. I don't know who's going to do all the work if Rick leaves, and he won't stay now that she's back. He's been offered a couple of positions already. I worry for my grandchild. She's not happy, and I seldom get to see her.'

Steph's heart gave a lurch. Rick had made his decision. Part of her was pleased he was not going back to live with Fiona, yet she didn't know why it mattered. She was still going back to her old life and Rick had no part in it.

'He never should have married that

girl. She was trouble right from the start.' Austin was still talking.

'They must have been happy at first,' she ventured.

'She made her mind up to get him, and in the end she succeeded. Fiona was very attractive. But she had a mouth on her and a temper to go with it. It wasn't long after they married that her father was taken ill and Rick was forced to take over. When he died Fiona inherited the whole place and she never let Rick forget it.'

He looked uncomfortable.

'I've been talking too much. Now let's have some of this tea, then we'll get your parcels back to your car.'

'Austin, what shall I do with the letters? Shall I bring them round to you?'

'No, dear. It would be too painful after all these years to read them. I rather hoped she'd destroyed them. But that wasn't Rose, was it?' He gave a sad smile and looked at her. 'Could I possibly ask you to destroy them for me? It would be a great weight off my mind.'

She put her hand on his arm.

'Of course.'

All the way home she couldn't stop thinking about what Rick would do. When she got back to the cottage she could hear the phone ringing as she opened the door and rushed to answer it. It was Bradley.

'Hello, Steph. I have a young couple interested in your cottage. They would like to come and see it now, if that would be OK with you.'

'Yes, yes, that's fine,' she heard herself saying.

At least the place looked its best after Rick's afternoon in the garden. He'd put more plants in and it looked like a proper cottage garden. She scattered the new cushions around and dumped the old ones in the bin. This young couple would be sure to like it.

They did. Jen Crabtree looked only in her early twenties and her husband not much older.

'I adore the kitchen,' she said. 'It's so cosy. And look at the garden!'

He was just as excited.

'You could plant an orchard out there, Jen.'

'And the living-room is just so homely. What wonderful beams.' She turned to Steph, her eyes shining. 'I love old places. They have a soul. You can feel all the people who've lived in them before you.'

They were equally enthralled with the bedroom, and when they peeped into the smaller one they looked at each other. It was so clear what they were thinking.

When they'd left she sat in the old chair and looked round and tried to see it through their eyes. Well, this could be it. They were young and had time and energy on their side, and they loved her cottage. They were a nice young couple and they would love it as she loved it.

It was the answer to her prayers. She could go back to London and get on with her life.

She went into the garden and sat on

the bench by the pond and watched as the sun slipped slowly behind the hedge and the sky turned scarlet.

Next morning Bradley phoned to say Mr and Mrs Crabtree wanted the cottage and were prepared to pay the asking price. Evidently they had inherited some money, so only needed a small mortgage which wouldn't pose a problem. They were fully aware of the state of it, but still loved it and would work at it together.

'Are you there, Steph?' She heard him say it three times and finally found her voice.

'Yes, I'm here. Yes, that's good.'

She was gripping the phone so hard her knuckles hurt. What was she saying? Bradley was talking all the time, but she wasn't listening. In the end she put the phone down and collapsed in the chair. Then she took several deep breaths and began to laugh and cry at the same time.

Then she flew out of the door and ran along the road to Elsie and Jim's house and almost fell inside their back door. But it wasn't Jim who caught hold of her. It was Rick.

She was so shocked it brought her back to her senses.

'What the matter?' Rick asked.

Steph realised how stupidly she was acting and pulled herself together but, unable to think of any way to extricate herself from the situation, she turned and fled. By the time she reached her cottage she was calmer. She closed the door in some relief and went into the kitchen. A cup of tea would steady her.

Rick had followed her back and was at the door. She let him in and tried to act calmly.

'Sorry about that. I wasn't expecting you to be there. I was hoping to see Jim about some work he's doing for me.' She was making it up as she went along, hoping to stall his questions and she succeeded. He gave her a puzzled look but seemed to accept it.

'You seemed a bit upset. Are you sure you're OK?'

'Absolutely. Couldn't be better. So off you go and get on with whatever you were doing.'

She wandered up to the shop, deep in thought. Bryony was there buying some milk, so Steph waited her turn behind the girl.

'So when's he off then?' Bel asked Bryony.

Bryony looked at the floor.

'I think he's going in a couple of weeks. Dad said that me and Mum will be living at Boland's now.'

'Are you pleased?' Bel asked.

Bryony nodded.

'Suppose so.' Then she left the shop.

'Poor kid,' Bel said. 'First she's carted off to Ormskirk, then back here. Then her dad's off to Cornwall. She doesn't know where she is most of the time.'

'Cornwall!' Steph could feel her heart thudding. What had she done? She had sold her cottage and let Rick go. She could have stopped him. He'd asked her to stay. They could have worked something out together.

As she walked down the lane, her heart was thumping as she admitted to herself that she wanted to stay. She wanted to stay and be with Rick. The shock of realisation knocked her sideways. She was in love. She had never felt this way before, and had been so determined never to, that she had denied the best thing that could ever have happened to her.

He had taken her at her word, given up on her and moved on. Now he had plans for a future. He had made his decision and she had no part to play in his new life. Tears welled in her eyes as she opened her door and, once safely in the privacy of the tiny hall, she stood with her back to the wall and wept out loud.

When the phone rang she knew it would be Greg and she didn't want to talk to him. It rang and rang. Eventually she could stand it no longer and picked up the receiver.

'Yes?' she snapped.

'Steph, where have you been? I've

been trying to get you all day.' It was Samantha from the office.

'I've been busy.'

'Steph, will you listen to me. It's important.'

Steph froze.

'What's wrong?'

'Nothing's wrong. In fact, it's amazing.'

'What's amazing? Samantha, do get on with it.'

'Oh, so you don't want to hear about a rumour that's going round the office about a certain person getting offered a top job, then?'

Steph was becoming irritated.

'Samantha, will you just spit it out for goodness' sake. I don't want to sit here all day.'

'Well.' Samantha's voice began to rise. 'I think you're in for a big promotion. I can't say more. Geoff wants to see you first thing Monday. So make sure you're here. From what I've heard it will be well worth the trouble.'

'OK, I'll be there.' She knew what

Samantha was like. There was probably nothing to get excited about. But she had nothing better to do and it might be worth her while.

'You don't seem that excited about it,' Samantha said.

'I'll find out what it's about first,' she said sensibly.

'OK, suit yourself.' And Samantha rang off.

Steph's heart was thumping at the possibility of it actually being the big one she'd been waiting for. If it was, she knew she wouldn't turn it down. It was the one thing she had always hoped for. Something really big to make all the effort worthwhile. Maybe, just maybe, this was it.

The Big One

The journey to London was long and Steph reached her flat tired and hot. As she tapped out the code at the entrance door and went to get in the lift, she was aware of someone behind her. She turned to see that Greg had followed her in and she could see from his look there was something not quite right.

'Steph, I've been waiting for you.'

'But why? I told you I'd phone you when I got back.'

'I'm afraid I have bad news.' He came towards her and put his hands on her shoulders and looked very solemn.

'What bad news?' Her heart started pumping, he looked so grave. 'What are you talking about?'

He led her inside to her flat. As he pushed the door open, she gasped. Everything was in chaos: drawers tipped out, chairs upturned, everything scattered everywhere.

He was still holding on to her hand.

'I came to make sure everything was OK for you coming home.' He hesitated. 'I found this. It's a good job you left your key with me or I wouldn't have been here.'

She walked from room to room in shock. Who would have done such a thing? Her whole life was in shreds on the floor. As she walked from room to room there seemed nothing that hadn't been rifled through.

Her voice sounded thin as she forced the words out.

'I don't understand. Who would do this? How did they even get as far as my door? Nobody can penetrate it without knowing the code. There are alarms everywhere.'

'It must be someone you know, Steph. Someone you've made an enemy of.' He looked stricken and she was grateful for his support.

'Can you think of anyone, Steph? It's all very sinister.'

She was near to tears, yet too shocked to succumb.

'I don't know. I thought I was safe here. This was the one place I felt safe.'

'You're never safe anywhere, Steph. It's something we have to live with, I'm afraid. When someone's intent on getting in, they can always find a way.'

Greg stood very close as they surveyed the shambles in the bedroom, and she could feel the strength of his protection. He was a real man, someone she could trust to care for her. He turned to face her and she let him engulf her in his arms, glad of the security they offered. Why had she underestimated how much he meant to her?

She sobbed into his shoulder. She could feel his arms tighten round her and they were silent for some minutes.

Finally she pulled away from him, her face ashen.

'But why? What did they want? I haven't anything valuable here. I can't think of anyone who'd do this to me.'

'Maybe it was jealousy. You're very successful. It's a competitive world we're in, Steph, easy to make enemies without intending to. A lot of men don't like women overtaking them in the workplace.'

This was even worse to contemplate. Was there someone she worked with who was capable of this? Someone who wanted what she had badly enough to trash her flat? Who would know the code to enter the building?

'Shall we call the police?' she asked.

He shook his head.

'Not yet. Let's tidy up and see if anything is missing.'

He began picking things up off the floor and piling them neatly on the bed.

'You check your jewellery and I'll look in the lounge. If we find something missing then we'll have to call the police in order for you to make a claim on your insurance.'

It did seem the simplest option and once they started it didn't take long. She didn't have a lot of stuff and it all seemed to be there and was soon put away in its place.

'Come on, now, let me take you out for dinner. Or would you rather I order a take-away?' Greg asked.

Greg was being very kind and gentle and she felt better now her flat was in order again. But even though it looked normal, it was tainted, and she was nervous wondering who had done it and why.

She opted for the take-away.

After some excellent food, they were both able to relax and conversation became more genial.

By ten o'clock she was finding it difficult to keep her eyes open and Greg got up from the table.

'You get off to bed; I can see you're worn out. I will come over in the morning and sort out the lock for you.'

She thanked him then bade him goodbye and headed to her bedroom. She soon realised she couldn't go to bed without sorting the front door. So she rang the locksmith, then changed the code on her security system. He arrived within the hour, examined the lock and told her it hadn't been broken at all and would still lock quite satisfactorily.

'Whoever did this unlocked the door first then tampered with it. The socket's been forced out, that's all. I can fix it.'

She frowned.

'No, change the lock. I won't feel safe unless you do.'

The man shook his head.

'Strange business. Looks like whoever did it just wanted you to think you'd been broken into.'

Once he'd gone, she phoned Greg to tell him she'd managed to get it fixed and that he didn't need to come next morning. To her surprise he was very put out.

'What did you do that for? I told you I'd fix it.'

'Well, it's fixed now. I appreciate you looking after the flat for me and helping sort it out. I'd have gone to pieces without your support. Now I have to get to bed. I've a long day ahead tomorrow.'

Next day Samantha was waiting for her as she walked through the door.

'Boss wants to see you straight away,' she told her, looking smug.

Geoff sat behind his desk working on his computer and told her to sit down. After what seemed like an age he looked up and peered at her over his spectacles.

'I have a proposition for you. Our Edinburgh branch is under-performing. We need someone up there to assess what the problem is and get things moving again. I've put your name forward for that job. How do you feel about it?'

'Edinburgh!' She felt her pulse quicken. That was one of their main branches. She knew there'd been trouble there and the manager had left under some sort of a cloud. The post had been left vacant for some time and the rumour was they couldn't find the right person to take it. And now it was being offered to her.

'You're asking me to move to Edinburgh?'

Geoff was giving her a strange look.

'Steph, I am asking you if you would be interested in managing the Edinburgh branch. It would mean an interview, of course. But I'm fairly certain you'd be offered the position. We don't have anyone else who could do the job as well as I know you could.'

She sat staring at him. This was an enormous promotion, one she could never have dreamed of. She opened her mouth but nothing came out.

'Steph, are you ill? I'm asking you if you would like this challenge. Are you interested?'

She wanted to jump up and hug him, but she tried to compose herself and think straight.

'Yes, I'll do it.' She was gripping her hands together on her lap and trying to stop her knees shaking.

He was still looking at her in a serious way.

'It's a big challenge. You realise that, don't you? It'll need all your energy and time.'

She didn't need him to tell her that. 'Geoff, I can do it.'

'Of course you can, which is why I suggested you for it. I have every confidence in you, Steph. I've booked you a flight for tomorrow morning so you can meet the team up there. No problem with that, I assume?'

'None at all. I'll go home and pack.' She had finally succeeded in getting control again and putting on the business-like exterior she felt appropriate to the occasion. Inside she was skipping and dancing and wanted to jump up and hug him. 'Thank you, Geoff.'

Excitement surged through her. Every other thought and feeling was wiped out. She was on her way to the top of her career. This was her big break.

She was impatient to be away from the flat she no longer felt safe in, away from people she no longer trusted, and away from all the worries of the cottage.

She met Greg for lunch at the café they often used, excited about telling him her exceptional news. He was waiting for her.

'How did it go?' he asked.

She was so bursting with pride and excitement she could hardly get it out.

'He's offered me Regional Manager of our Edinburgh branch,' she squeaked.

'I hope you told him you wouldn't go,' he said.

She couldn't believe his reaction to her news.

'Of course I'm going. Aren't you happy for me?'

'Of course I want you to advance in your career. But you can't just up sticks and leave everything on a whim.'

She stood up and grabbed her coat angrily.

'It's not a whim. This is my future and if you can't be happy for me then I fear our friendship is over.' Anger had replaced all her happiness. She felt drained and deflated.

People at tables round them were

beginning to notice there was something wrong and were looking. Steph had never felt so uncomfortable. All she wanted was to escape and get back to her flat and be on her own.

She walked out of the café closely followed by a blustering Greg. Once outside she turned to him.

'Greg, please leave me alone. I want to go home and have some time to myself. I don't want hassle. You have no business telling me what I should or should not do.'

He was looking worried now.

'I'm sorry, Steph. I only wanted to advise you. You know I always have your best interests at heart.'

'I don't think you do,' she said, turning away and walking quickly towards the tube station, leaving him staring after her.

Sitting in the train she went over the offer she had been given. A lot of the initial excitement had worn off now after her confrontation with Greg, and she began to think about the reality of the situation. Was she ready for such a move? She wasn't sure she could cope in a new city away from everything and everyone she knew all on her own.

She slept badly that night, her dreams taking her back to the cottage. She woke early and lay in bed thinking about it all. Such a tiny community, so few people, yet so comfortable. There was sadness, yes, but she preferred that to the cold indifference she felt here. Even Greg wasn't really interested in her. He wanted her to be what he thought she ought to be.

The fact was that Rick was moving on and she couldn't deny him his one chance of freedom to follow his dream, as she was about to follow hers. Once he had gone, the place wouldn't be the same. This would be a new start for both of them. She would go back to the cottage as soon as she could, get the furniture moved out and say goodbye.

Rick phoned that afternoon and she was delighted to hear his voice.

'Steph, I tried to see you before you

left. I wanted to tell you my plans. I'm living with Dad for the time being. But I've found my ideal job. It's on a big estate in Cornwall. I could be head gardener when the old chap retires, and there's a house to go with it. And I was wondering — '

His voice tailed away and she didn't tell him she already knew about this.

'Rick, I'm so happy for you. You were wasting your time at that place. I've got some news, too. I've been offered Regional Manager in Edinburgh.'

'That's wonderful news.' His voice sounded forced.

'So who's going to run Boland's now?' She wanted to keep him talking for as long as possible. It was so good to be in touch with him again and hear him happy.

'Fiona will. She'll be OK. She's always been good with the books and orders. She has two good workers and she can employ casual labour in the summer. There's always plenty of people looking for that. I couldn't carry on there. It would have been an impossible situation.'

'What about Bryony?'

'That's the bit that hurts. But I feel it's best all round if I leave. I've spoken to Bryony about it and she understands. She's a sensible girl.'

'Well, good luck with the new job.' She could hardly get the words out for the tremble in her voice.

There was a pause. Neither of them wanted the call to end, but there seemed little else to say.

'Will you be coming up to the cottage again?' he asked.

She tried to explain the situation, but was so near to tears her voice was wavering.

'I expect you will have gone by the time I do come back,' she finally managed.

'Can't you come soon? I really want to see you.'

'No, my boss has made it very clear he thinks I'm taking too much time off work. I have to go up to Edinburgh tomorrow to meet the team up there.'

'That's some way to go from London. Will you drive?'

'I have a flight booked for six in the morning. I'll probably be done by lunchtime.'

'What, you fly up in the morning and then back after lunch?'

'No, I persuaded Geoff to let me stay over in the Grand Hotel. That's where the meeting is. I'm planning on a shopping trip on Princes Street to celebrate.'

'I see,' he said. 'Well, happy shopping then.'

There didn't seem much else to say so they rang off.

The meeting went well next day. Steph liked the others and felt she could work with them. She could immediately pinpoint the problem areas and what had to be done to improve the performance of the branch and she was sure she would have co-operation from the team.

There would be interviews to get

through, but she sensed they would be a formality as Geoff had indicated. When Geoff made a decision, others didn't argue with him.

It was three o'clock when she came out of the meeting, so she went up to her room to change from her formal suit into something more casual when the bedside phone rang. It was reception telling her there was someone wanting to talk to her.

She took the call and was delighted to hear Rick's voice.

'Rick, how nice to hear from you again.'

'Steph, have you finished your meeting? I want to meet you.'

'Rick, I'm in Edinburgh.'

'So am I.'

She stared into the phone.

'What, where?' Even to herself she sounded stupid.

'Just downstairs in the lobby.'

'What?' She was confused.

'Come on, now. You usually manage more than two words at a time.'

'You're in this hotel?'

'I am here and waiting for you. Unless you have some wealthy client awaiting your pleasure.' He sounded on top of the world.

'I'll come down. No, you come up. See you in five minutes.'

Rick was laughing at her as she put the phone down.

Steph was laughing as she scrambled into a pair of white trousers and loose flowery tunic. He was here. She would be with him in minutes. Nothing else in the world mattered.

He hugged her and gave her a tentative kiss. Then he took her hand and and pulled her outside into the lobby.

'Where are we going?' she asked.

'I'll explain when we get in the car.'

As they drove out of town, Rick explained where they were off to.

'It's a big estate. My friend is head gardener. We were at college together. So when I knew you were coming here, I decided to pay him a long overdue visit and see you at the same time. He's doing what I've always wanted to do.'

'Does he know I'm coming, too?'

'Yes, he's looking forward to meeting you. They all are. He has a wife and three children.'

'So, what about this new job of yours?'

'Ah, yes, Cornwall.' He was silent for a moment and the sideways glance he gave told her he'd noticed the quaver in her voice and knew what she was feeling.

'It's a beautiful part of the country. I'd be looking after the gardens for a country hotel. I'd get to put my own ideas into place. There's accommodation to go with the job.'

'So, when do you start?'

'It hasn't reached that stage yet. They've offered me the job, but I haven't accepted it yet. It's a big move and I wanted to consider all my options first.'

Steph was surprised. She'd thought that Rick had accepted the job, but now it seemed that nothing was confirmed.

Oakfield Manor was just a few miles outside Edinburgh and, as they wound down the curving tree-lined drive, the beautiful stone building came into view. The path curved round behind some stable blocks and then into a courtyard where Rick parked his car. There was a smaller building to the side and a pleasant-looking woman about Steph's age came out and called to them.

'You found us, then. Now come away in and let me see you,' she said.

Rick introduced Steph to Katie, then Katie turned back to him.

'Well, now, Rick, how good to see you again.' She hugged him and then turned back to Steph. 'It's years now since I last saw this man. We were good friends back in those days. All students together. Andrew will be in soon. He had some business to attend to.'

She took them through into a light airy room overlooking a lovely walled garden.

'You've a grand place here,' Rick

said. 'Andrew certainly fell on his feet getting this job.'

'Yes, we like it well enough. Madam's a bit of a pain at times, but Andrew has her measured. She knows what she wants and insists on having it.'

Andrew came in shortly after and he and Rick were obviously delighted to see each other again and chatted enthusiastically about the estate and old times at college.

'Why don't I show you around?' Andrew said to Rick. 'Would you like to come, Steph, or would you rather sit in the garden for a while and chat with Katie?'

'They'll be talking shop all the time,' Katie warned her. 'We could take a walk later, if you like. First, I think a cup of tea might be in order.'

Steph warmed to Katie immediately.

'I'd love that,' she said. 'Just to relax in the garden would be wonderful.'

Katie made the tea and carried the tray out into the garden, where there was a selection of comfortable chairs arranged round a table. Steph sank into one of them and a wave of happiness washed over her.

Rick and Andrew came back eventually and Rick looked happier than she had ever seen him. He plonked himself down in the chair next to Steph and took her hand.

'Steph. I have to take you to see the gardens. There are orchards and the most beautiful lake.'

Katie watched them.

'Do you have to rush off? Why not stay and enjoy a few days in the countryside. We have plenty of bedrooms, as you can see. It's an enormous house even for five of us.'

Rick looked at Steph.

'Could we do that?'

The sun was warm on her face and the way Rick held her hand felt so good. She wanted to stay here with these lovely people more than anything. She wanted her time with Rick to last. Reluctantly, she turned to him.

'I have a hotel room booked for

tonight,' she said.

'Could we possibly cancel it?' he asked tentatively.

She made an instant decision. Whatever the outcome, she was going to have this special time.

'Don't see why not. I have a few days' grace before I have to report back to the office. So long as you don't mind me sending a few e-mails.'

'How about you, Rick? Don't have to get back in a hurry, do you?' Andrew said.

'No, I can stay a day or two. I'd like to see more of what you're doing here.'

'Well, that's settled,' Katie said. 'Steph can use the office. Andrew and Rick can catch up on old times. I'll cook dinner and we can have a relaxing evening together.'

'I need to pick up my case from the hotel,' Steph said.

'Of course! Silly me.' Katie was thoughtful. 'Do you think you can manage tonight? I can provide you with most of the essentials, then tomorrow we could pick up your stuff and go shopping in Edinburgh. What do you say?'

'That would be fine. I want to see Princes Street.'

'Good. It will be a treat for me, too. We can leave the men to their own devices for the day and I'm sure they'll be delighted to be rid of us.'

They stayed for three days. Geoff was pleased with the report Steph sent.

'Good girl, I knew you were the right person for the job,' he told her over the phone.

Rick was in his element, following Andrew round the estate and seeing how everything worked. They met Lady Margaret. She was an elderly lady, who had been widowed for several years, loved her estate and kept a close eye on her gardeners. But Andrew seemed to respect her and she obviously adored him.

'She knows what she wants,' he told them. 'And she knows what she's talking about.'

Steph and Rick would walk around the estate together when the family had other things to do. They were comfortable together and Steph felt she had known Rick all her life. Conversation was easy as they exchanged views and ideas.

'You really like it here, don't you?' Steph asked as they strolled round the lake. 'I could see you doing this job. Boland's was so wrong for you.'

'I'm not aiming quite so high. This is a huge estate. I'm not ready for this yet.'

'At least you will finally be doing what you enjoy. I really hope it works out for you. Won't you miss all the folk in the village?'

He squeezed her hand.

'I'll miss one of them very much.' He paused. 'You really care, don't you, Steph?' He stopped and looked at her. 'Fiona only saw me as a useful person to have about the place. She couldn't see why I hated the work, thought I ought to have been grateful for a ready-made job.'

Steph was looking into those gentle blue eyes and her heart twisted in pain.

'I've never thought of work like that. I couldn't do a job I didn't enjoy.'

He held her gaze.

'You're lucky. You've always known what you wanted and gone for it. I've spent too much time dithering.'

'You've always known what you want. It's just taken you a little longer to get there.'

'Yes, I know what I want. Whether I will ever get there is another matter,' he said and he took her hand again and they continued their walk.

She needed to lighten the conversation. The tightness inside her was becoming stifling.

'I've loved my job ever since I started. It can be a bit stressful, especially when you have a boss like Geoff,' she said, forcing a small laugh.

'Don't you get on with him?' Rick seemed relieved the conversation had taken a lighter turn.

'I respect him. He's very good at his job. I just think he worries too much and gets everyone else in the same state.'

He looked at her.

'I can't see you being like that. I bet you're as cool as a cucumber.'

She raised an eyebrow.

'Is that how you see me? Cool and aloof?'

'I suppose to some extent. You always seem to be in control of your life. Not like me. I'm always trying to keep everyone happy. And it's very difficult at times.'

She didn't know how to take this and she thought about what Simon had once said about her not needing anyone, always being self sufficient. She never saw herself like that. Maybe they were right.

Rick put his arm round her shoulder.

'Let's get back. They'll be wondering where we are.'

She let him lead her round the lake to the path, his arm round her and her head resting on his chest. He pulled her closer, then he stopped and turned her towards him.

'You're a very special woman,' he said. 'I very much want to kiss you.' She lifted her face and his lips closed over hers as his arms enfolded her. They stood for a long time, both lost in the closeness of each other.

Her flight home came all too soon. Rick set off in his car after seeing her to the airport. There had been no mention of meeting up again. It seemed an unspoken agreement that they wouldn't.

She went back to her flat and almost immediately Greta rang.

'Where have you been hiding? I haven't seen you since the barbecue. I want all the news.'

'Greta, I'm exhausted. Can we leave it for another time?'

'Oh, come on, Steph. Just a quick drink at Brown's. It'll do you good. You sound a bit down.'

She did feel down. Brown's was a new bar only a couple of blocks away.

She could cope with that, and Greta was always a tonic.

'OK, you win. See you in half an hour. But I'm not staying long. I've had a tiring day and I have to be in the office at eight in the morning.'

The bar was busy, but they found a table in a corner where they could talk.

'Now, is it true that you're going up to Edinburgh?' Greta asked.

'Wow, the bush telegraph is efficient,' Steph said.

'You know nothing stays a secret for long among our crowd. Greg's not too pleased. He's been like a bear with a sore head since he found out. In fact, I wanted to talk to you about Greg — and about the break-in.'

'Greta, I came here to be cheered up, not depressed. Look, nothing was taken. I've had new locks put on and I'm not going to be there much longer. I'm not worried about it any more.'

'Didn't you think it was odd that nothing was damaged or missing?'

'Yes, I did. But what was more

strange was the lock. It had been damaged *after* it was opened. None of it makes sense. I'd rather not think about it.'

'Well, I've thought about it. I've been thinking about it ever since you rang me that night.'

'And what have you come up with?'

'You said everything was there and nothing damaged. Whoever got in made it look like the lock had been forced.'

'Yes, that's right. Very strange.'

'And you said Greg didn't want you to contact the police, and he didn't want you to get the locksmith. He just happened to be there when you got home.'

'Yes . . .'

'Steph, you're not stupid. It's staring you in the face.'

She felt a cold chill creep through her.

'You think Greg did it?'

'Yes, I do. It all fits. He doesn't like you going off to the cottage all the time. He thinks this will frighten you into staying put, protecting your property, and wanting him there to protect you. He's desperate.'

'No, Greta. He wouldn't do that. That's a terrible thing to think. Greg might be a pain, but he's a decent man.'

'Decent men do some pretty crazy things when they're obsessed. And Greg is obsessed with you, sweetie.'

'No, I'm not going to believe this.'

'Right, suit yourself. But tell me, why did you let him have your key? You've never let him have it before.'

'He told me there'd been a spate of burglaries in the area and he thought it best if he kept an eye on the place while I was spending so much time at the cottage.'

As she said it she realised Greta was right, and knew with absolute certainty that Greg had done it. Never in her life had she felt so betrayed. Nothing she had ever experienced came close to the feeling she had now.

Greta saw her distress.

'I'm sorry I had to put you in the

picture, but I think you know I'm right.'

'Yes, Greta, you're right. I hadn't realised how far this had gone. He really is a dangerous man.'

'I wouldn't put it like that, but it has to be dealt with.'

They finished their drink and walked back to Greta's car.

'I'll give you a lift home. Or would you rather come back with me?'

'No, I'll be all right, Greta. But thank you.'

When she let herself into her flat she felt it was tainted. Everything about her life was tainted. All she could think about was her cottage and Rick, and she focused on that as she fell asleep.

She awoke next morning feeling stronger and determined to confront Greg. He answered his phone on the second ring.

'Steph, how nice to hear from you. I didn't realise you were going to be away so long. What kept you? I hope there isn't a problem with the new job.'

He was trying to sound pleasant, but

the insincerity rang through until she could listen no longer.

'Greg. I need to see you. Can you come round now? It's urgent.' This needed to be done face to face so that he couldn't hang up on her. She needed to see his reaction.

'Of course.' He sounded pleased to have been asked. 'I was on my way to the bank, but I'll phone and tell them I've been delayed. I'll be with you in no time.'

He looked full of himself when she opened the door to him and she stepped aside to let him in, her face stony. He moved to kiss her cheek but she backed off.

'So, what's the problem?' he asked.

'The problem is that I know who broke into my flat.'

The expression on his face showed her all she needed to know, but he said nothing.

'I know it was you, Greg.'

He became agitated, walking towards the living-room, his hands clenching and unclenching. Then he turned towards her.

'What are you talking about? Why would I do that? I had a key. You gave it to me. What are you talking about?'

She stood perfectly still in the hallway and he stood facing her, red faced and jumpy.

'I'm talking about you and me. We are finished, Greg. I don't want to see you again. Please leave this flat, never come back and do not try to contact me.'

He shook his head.

'You're upset about something. Let's talk about this. You can't believe I would do such a thing.' He was coming closer to her and she pulled her phone from her pocket.

'Yes, I do. Now are you going to leave?'

He stood there, running his hands through his hair then shook his head.

'You're stressed over the new job. I knew it wouldn't be right for you. And this cottage as well. It's too much for you. You don't know what you're saying. OK, I'm going.'

Once he was out she locked the door and leaned against it, wishing with all her heart she wasn't there any more.

Return to the Cottage

By Friday the pull of the motorway was all consuming. She'd told Geoff she needed time off to sort things out for Edinburgh and this time he hadn't argued.

'What are you going to do with the cottage?' Greta asked when she called round to tell her about Greg. 'You seem a bit edgy. You're not rushing off, I hope.'

Greta went over to the patio window and sat in one of the armchairs and Steph sat opposite to her. The view across Hampstead Heath was calming and she relaxed in the luxury of her surroundings. Greta's house always had that effect on her.

She spoke without taking her eyes from the view.

'It's all going through. I just want to make the most of it while I still have it.'

'Are you having second thoughts about Edinburgh?'

Steph looked at her in surprise.

'No. I've said I'll do it. I'm a bit apprehensive, but I think that's normal. It's a big responsibility. And I won't know anyone there.'

'You didn't know anyone here when you first came,' Greta reminded her.

It was true, but then she'd been young and full of confidence.

'That's true. I'll be fine. It's just nerves kicking in. I'm all sorted here and now I have to start again.'

'Look, why don't you go to your cottage and take a few days to think it through? Geoff can't expect you to make a decision like that overnight.'

'I already have. I told him I'd do it.'

'You can always tell him you've changed your mind.'

'Greta, why are you talking like this? I thought you'd have been all for it. You've never let anything stop you.'

'I've known you a long time and I know something's wrong. You're not happy about this move, are you?'

Steph sighed and gave a wan smile.

'You know me too well. I can't hide anything from you.' Steph sat silently staring at her hands. Then she looked up at Greta and shook her head, misery etched on her features. 'I don't know. That place seems to have got into my blood. I've never felt like this before.'

Greta gave her a knowing look.

'I think it's the man that's got into your blood. It's not the job, is it? Steph, be honest. It's Rick. He's unsettled you. I've never seen you like this before.'

Steph could feel the tears coming and sniffed hard to try to stop them. Her hands wouldn't stop trembling. Greta saw her distress and put an arm around her shoulder.

'Spill the beans. No good bottling it all up.'

Steph gripped her hands in her lap and swallowed to try to keep calm.

'I can't let it happen, Greta. We both have plans and they're taking us in different directions. I need to re-focus on my career, then I'll be OK.'

The tears were spilling over now and she couldn't stop them. Greta rubbed her back to try to comfort her.

'Come on, sweetie. What is it you really want?'

Steph straightened up and tried to take control. With supreme effort she stared through the window without seeing anything.

'I wish I could go to my cottage and stay there and never have to make another decision in my life. But it isn't going to happen. I have to move on and this is the best offer I'm likely to have. So I'm going to take it and get on with it.'

Greta frowned and felt the tension in Steph as she tried to get a grip on herself.

'You don't have to. You could stay in your cottage and still do your job. You're good at it, Steph. You could work anywhere, even set up on your own. It's your choice. Don't let anyone bully you into making the wrong one.'

'Greta, stop it. I've made my decision. There's nothing more to discuss.' She stood up purposefully and straightened to her full height, then shook herself and arranged a smile on her face. 'I need a cup of coffee.'

Greta reluctantly left it at that and went into the kitchen to put on the coffee. When Steph made up her mind about something, nothing would shake her out of it. But she was fearful her friend was making a bad mistake.

After three hours in a traffic jam Steph was stiff and weary when she unfolded herself from the car at the cottage. She had hardly closed the door and put on the lights when the knock came. Rick stood sheepishly on the doorstep and smiled at her.

'I know it's late, but I had to see you.'

It all happened so quickly. One minute she was standing to let him in and the next the door was closed and she was in his arms. Everything melted away as she gave herself to the moment. Whatever followed didn't matter. She had this moment, and as he enveloped her in the warmth of his body, the world melted away.

They remained locked together for a long time before he closed his lips over hers and that wonderful feeling of coming home turned to longing, and a certainty of knowing this was where she wanted to be. When they pulled apart their eyes locked.

'I wanted to show you how I feel about you. Now it's up to you.'

'How did you know I was here? I only arrived a few minutes ago.'

'I've driven past the cottage every day in the hope of seeing your car. I knew you'd be back.'

When he left she stared at the night through the window and watched him climb into his car, hugging herself in sheer happiness. She wouldn't let her mind dwell on the future tonight and eventually she slipped into bed in a rosy glow and almost immediately was asleep.

Next morning was different. What had Rick meant that it was up to her?

She was in turmoil all morning, couldn't settle to the paperwork she'd brought with her, couldn't find what she was looking for on her laptop. She didn't answer the phone and turned her mobile off. Eventually she gave up and went for a walk.

It was silly. Her life wasn't here. She was about to start a new job in Edinburgh and he was off down to Cornwall. Rick had commitments, a family. She had a career. It had all gone wrong once for both of them and it could happen again, and she wasn't going to take that chance.

When she did eventually answer his call she told him so and he didn't argue. He came round to see her.

'Steph, my past is past.'

'But Fiona still has a hold over you. You do what she wants all the time. Why don't you stand up to her, tell her she can't just turn you out because she wants you to come back. I don't understand why you put up with it.'

He shook his head and looked angry.

'I do what's best for my daughter.'

She was silent, knowing she'd gone too far. She would never understand the situation and she should have kept her mouth shut. She should also have known that Rick was no pushover. He cared for his daughter and he'd put her first.

'I'm sorry. I shouldn't have said that. It's none of my business. We're both moving on. I have my life and you have yours. Can we part as friends?'

'Is that what you want?'

'We've had good times. Let's not spoil it by arguing.'

'Do you really want to sell your cottage?' he asked. 'I don't think it's what you want. You keep coming back.'

Steph frowned.

'I've been trying to sell it and I have to keep an eye on it.'

'No, you don't. You come here because you want to.'

She said nothing and he continued.

'I don't know much about your life in London, who your friends are, what you do when you're not working. All you ever talk about is the time you lived here, your happy childhood. What's happened in your life since then? I can see the difference in you when you've been here a day or two. The city girl disappears and the real Steph comes through. You belong here.'

She shook her head.

'No, I don't. I'm just that strange upstart from London who comes here and causes problems.'

She regretted saying it the minute she saw the look on his face.

'What are you talking about?'

She was flustered now.

'Oh, nothing. Look, I really do have things to do.'

'Not until you've explained what you mean. I have the feeling this has something to do with me.'

She could see he was determined.

'I seem to have upset Fiona and Bel. All these women in your life and then I come along and rock the boat.' She tried a weak smile.

He sighed and shook his head.

'Bel's a lovely person and I help her out when I can as she's on her own. But I'm careful not to let her think there's anything more to it than that, because I know how she feels towards me.'

'But you tell her things you don't share with me, like your future plans. I heard of those first in her shop. It was days later before you told me.'

'Yes, I confide in Bel. I needed someone to talk to about what I was doing. I've known her a long time and she's easy to talk to.'

'And I'm not, is that it?'

There was anger in his look.

'When you're in this mood, no.'

They stood glaring at each other. Eventually he turned and went out of the back door, leaving her deflated and empty.

* * *

Geoff was on the phone constantly, trying to get Steph to commit to dates for her move to Edinburgh.

'We need a decision. Steph. The branch needs a manager and if you don't want to do it we have to find someone else.

She did want to do it. She knew she'd be good at it, could turn it round. But her heart was heavy knowing how much distance she was putting between herself and Rick, and with memories of their disagreement.

The night she'd arrived and he'd held her and kissed her, he'd said it was up to her. Yet, she hadn't asked him what he meant and still wasn't sure. Maybe Bel was right. If she stayed then maybe he would. But then he'd be giving up his one chance of the job he wanted to do. And there would always be the shadow of Fiona lurking.

'Can you give me a few more days?' she asked Geoff.

It was a lovely evening and she was reluctant to go inside so wandered into the garden. The geraniums were in full bloom, the hydrangea bushes full of colour and the roses climbing round the corner of the cottage smelled wonderful. The grass was neat and now she could sit by the pond on her new bench and watch the fish she'd put into it swimming between the water lilies.

Rick had cleaned up the pebble dash and even the window-sills looked better with a coat of paint.

There was movement in the shed, she was sure of it. There it was again. She got up and moved nearer to the shed window. Nothing. She sat down and saw it again, something white just inside the glass. Cautiously she went and peered through the window. She couldn't see anything but she could hear something. It sounded like a child sobbing. She opened the shed door and saw Bryony crouched on the floor, her head in her hands.

Steph stood watching and said nothing. Eventually Bryony looked up, her face stony, her eyes red rimmed. Steph kneeled beside her but the girl didn't move.

'Bryony, what's wrong?' she asked gently.

Bryony stood up and tried to edge past her but Steph barred her way.

'Where are you going? Come in the house.'

Bryony tried to push her aside.

'No, you'll only make me go back. I'm not going back there. Dad's going away, and he won't take me with him. You can't make me do anything.'

She was working herself into a frenzy. Steph had no experience in dealing with young girls and was afraid this one was going to slip away and come to harm if she didn't stop her.

They stood in the shed facing each other.

'Bryony, I am not going to make you do anything you don't want to do. You can stay in my shed for as long as you please. But I have a spare bedroom which is much more comfortable.'

Bryony stopped and looked at her.

'You won't tell them where I am? You'll let me stay?'

Steph could see no alternative. She had to keep the girl with her, and safe.

'Can we go inside and talk about it?'

Slowly Bryony followed her into the cottage and as they sat at the kitchen table Steph gradually calmed her and they began to talk.

'Where's your mum?' Steph asked her.

'She's at home.'

'Why don't we phone her, then,' Steph suggested. 'Just let her know you're safe?'

It was a mistake. Bryony was on her feet and through the back door and Steph only just caught hold of her.

'It was only a suggestion. If you don't want me to contact her, I won't. But your mum and dad will be worried when they find you're missing.'

'No, they won't. They don't care about me. They just keep shouting at each other. At least Mum shouts and then Dad walks out. I'm not going back.'

'OK, you're safe here. Tell me what

this is all about. Why were you hiding in my shed?'

Bryony looked at Steph and eventually decided she could trust her.

'I had to get out. They keep shouting at each other. I couldn't stand it any more so I ran out.'

Steph saw the hurt in her eyes. She seemed so lost and vulnerable, and she had so much of Rick about her. Steph put an arm round her shoulder.

'Come on, sweetheart. You look tired.'

She found an old T-shirt for Bryony to sleep in, made her a hot drink and tucked her into Rose's freshly made bed.

'You won't tell them where I am, will you?'

Steph knew she couldn't promise that, but she didn't want Bryony rushing off into the night, the state she was in.

'Look, sweetheart, we have to let them know you're safe, but I will keep you here tonight, so you go to sleep. In the morning we'll decide what is to be done.'

Bryony seemed too tired to argue. Before Steph was out of the room her eyes were closed. She must have been completely exhausted.

Steph sat for a long time wondering what she should do. There was an urgent knocking at the door and Rick stood there, white faced. Before he even spoke Steph told him Bryony was safely in her bed.

He visibly relaxed and followed her into her front room.

'I've been looking all afternoon. Nobody's seen her. I've searched the whole village.'

'Except my shed,' Steph said and smiled at him to try to cheer him up.

He gave her a relieved smile; then it disappeared.

'Why did she do it?'

Steph explained how she'd found Bryony and what she'd said. Rick listened, his face serious.

'Shall I get her and take her back with me?'

Steph shook her head.

'She's sound asleep. There's no point in waking her now. Let her stay and come for her in the morning.'

'Are you sure?'

'Look, she didn't want me to tell you where she was. She tried to make me promise. I'm sorry I didn't let you know, but she wouldn't have stayed if I had and she was in such a state I didn't want her running off again. She trusts me.' Guilt was overwhelming her. She expected Rick to be rightfully angry with her and was surprised he wasn't.

'I wonder why she came here. Fiona phoned me as soon as she found she was missing.'

'She seemed very distressed about all the arguing. I think she thought my shed looked like a peaceful place to hide.'

'It's difficult for her, I know. I wish Fiona wouldn't go on the way she does in front of her. The poor kid doesn't know where she is.'

He looked weary and she felt for him. 'Go home and get some rest. She's safe here. I'll take good care of her, don't worry.'

'I know you will. Thank you, Steph. I'll go and put Fiona's mind at rest and then get back to Dad. We'll talk in the morning.'

Steph was up early next morning but there was no sound from Bryony. When she looked into the bedroom she was sleeping soundly. She was a pretty girl when she wasn't scowling, her dark hair falling in silken strands on the pillow. Steph smiled and quietly pulled the door to. She'd leave her in peace until Rick came.

But it was Fiona who came for her.

'Shush, she's fast asleep,' Steph told her.

'I'll give her fast asleep. I'm supposed to be in Liverpool today. I don't know what I'm going to do now — drag her along with me, I suppose. Can't leave her at home if she's going to act like this. Why's she here, anyway?'

Steph was taken aback. She didn't want another confrontation, especially as Bryony was asleep upstairs.

Fiona was still raging.

'Well, let's have her. I thought her father was coming for her, but he's busy with some supplier on the phone. I'm always the one to have to deal with her.'

Fiona seemed genuinely distressed and Steph felt that beneath the bluster there was a troubled woman.

'Come in for a cup of tea and I'll get her.'

Fiona stared at her.

'Please, I've just boiled the kettle.' Steph stood aside for her to come in.

'Well, if you're sure.' All the steam had drained from her as she followed Steph into the kitchen and sat at the table while Steph made the tea.

'You've made a big improvement in this place,' Fiona said, looking round.

Steph handed Fiona a mug and sat opposite her at the kitchen table.

'Had to. No-one would have bought it the state it was in. I've only cleaned it up. There's still a lot to do. At least we've got the garden straight.'

The minute she'd said it she knew it was a mistake. Fiona's face hardened again. Then she sighed and to Steph's surprise her face crumpled and a tear ran down her cheek.

Steph didn't know what to do.

'I'm sorry,' she repeated, feeling sorry for her. She knew that feeling when all the world seemed to be going wrong for you. 'I really didn't know anything about you when Rick first came to do my garden. I didn't know anything about him, either. I wouldn't have let him do the greenhouse with your glass if I'd known.'

'No, it's me that's wrong. I always antagonise people. Nobody in the village likes me. Just because I was a wild teenager. They're very narrow minded in this village. That's why I left. Wanted to get away from it all.' Fiona brushed the tears away and blew her nose. 'But I'm back now, and they're not going to chase me away again. That's my place and I'm staying, what-ever they say.'

'But what about Rick? It's a bit hard on him, isn't it?' Steph could have bitten off her tongue. Here she was talking out of turn, interfering in things she knew nothing of. She waited for the onslaught. But it didn't come.

Instead Fiona looked at her seriously.

'No, Rick's fine about it. He agrees it's best for all of us. He's always accepted it's my place. He hates being there, always has. Only too pleased to be released from it and free to go off and do his own thing.' Bitterness crept into her voice. 'At last we've actually agreed on something.'

This was a surprise.

'But Bryony said she ran away because you were shouting at each other.'

'We were, but it had nothing to do with that. He was mad because I'd upset our workers. He told me they were threatening to leave and he felt this was unfair, as they'd worked so hard to pull the place together when I left. Anyway, I talked to them and they've agreed to stay on. I just have to keep control of my temper.'

'I see,' Steph said again. All these revelations took a bit of taking in.

Fiona's face crumpled again and she looked at Steph.

'Rick's a good man, you know.'

'Yes, he is,' Steph said. She could tell this was costing Fiona dearly.

'I made a mistake leaving. The grass is always greener, you know. We rubbed along well enough when I look back. He's hard working and reliable. But I wanted more.' She gave a hollow laugh. 'Well, I got it all right. Now Rick doesn't want anything to do with me. I don't blame him. I messed up and now I have to live with it.' She stood up. 'I'd better get her, then, and I'll cancel my appointment. By the time I get her organised it'll be too late.'

Steph saw her opportunity.

'Why don't you leave her here? She's no trouble and then you can go to Liverpool as planned and I can take her home when she wakes up.'

Fiona looked at her.

'Are you sure? I don't want to stop you getting on. I know you have a lot on your plate with this place.'

'I'm sure.'

It was the first time she had seen Fiona smile. It was a tentative smile but it transformed her face.

Bryony Helps Steph

Bryony slept until midday, then appeared bedraggled at the kitchen door. Steph was sorting out washing to go into the machine.

'Want some breakfast? Or is it lunchtime?'

'Not hungry,' was the reply she got.

'I've some fresh rolls, and I've eggs in the fridge.'

'I told you I'm not hungry,' Bryony mumbled.

'I'm afraid I can't offer you the luxury of a shower, but there's plenty of hot water for a bath if you fancy a soak.'

Bryony said nothing but turned and went back upstairs. Steph heard the water running and left her to it. It was a long time before she appeared again. Steph was in the garden up a ladder, trying to reach the top branches of a tall pine tree. She stopped working when she saw Bryony.

'Do you want me to take you home now?' she asked.

Bryony was studying the tree.

'No, I can walk.'

Steph wasn't too happy about that. What if Bryony decided to wander off again? She'd assured Rick she would take care of her and told Fiona she would take her home.

'Shall we go to the shop first and get you something to eat? I'm afraid I don't know what young girls like to eat.'

'We eat the same as everyone else,' Bryony said, still staring up at the tree.

Steph raised an eyebrow.

'In that case I'm going to warm up some soup and have it with the rolls. Does that appeal?'

'OK,' Bryony said.

Steph went into the kitchen and got the pan out of the cupboard. She warmed the rolls and set places at the table. When she looked out of the window she was alarmed to see Bryony at the top of the step ladder with the saw. She held her breath and watched as she expertly sawed the top off the tree and it tumbled to the ground. Then Bryony came down the ladder and began to saw the huge branch into smaller pieces.

Steph went out to her.

'That was pretty impressive,' she said.

The girl shrugged.

'Done it before. Me and Dad used to do lots like this before we went away.'

'Do be careful,' Steph said as Bryony continued to saw the pieces. 'Why don't you just leave it now? I've got lunch ready.'

'You can't leave it like that. Dad won't be able to get it into the trailer if you don't make the pieces smaller.'

'No, I suppose not.'

Steph held the branches steady as Bryony told her to and Bryony sawed away with expertise. Soon the whole lot was in a neat pile ready for collection.

'Shall we eat now?' Steph said.

'OK.' Bryony wandered towards the kitchen door.

The soup was only warm but Bryony ate it without complaint and finished all the rolls.

Bryony stayed well into the afternoon and they were now clearing some weed that was clogging the pond.

'Why don't you put some proper aquatic plants in it?' Bryony asked.

'Maybe I will.' Steph said.

They stared into the water together. Bryony pointed excitedly.

'Look, there's a frog in there.'

Steph peered in the direction she was pointing, then bent down to look under the stone.

'I see it. Fancy that. I thought they only went into water during the breeding season.'

'They like damp places. He probably lives in this garden.'

Steph stood up straight and stretched her back. Then she saw Rick. He was standing by the side of the house smiling at them. Bryony saw him, too, and waved.

He ambled over.

'You two seem to be enjoying yourselves.'

Bryony shrugged.

'That wood needs moving, Dad,' she said.

Rick nodded his agreement.

'I'd better get the trailer then.'

They loaded the branches on to the trailer.

'If we piled the logs by the shed you could burn them on the fire in the winter,' Bryony said to Steph.

Rick looked at Steph and she could read his mind.

'Let's do that,' she said.

'I'll do it. Dad never gets them right.' Bryony already had an armful.

Steph glanced at Rick, who was watching his daughter with amusement.

'OK, I'll make us a cup of tea.'

Rick followed her into the kitchen. Steph dunked a couple of tea bags while Rick watched her.

They sat on the patio and drank their tea, watching Bryony stacking the logs. Then Rick got up to go.

'Let's get you home. I'm sure Steph has things to do.'

Bryony looked up with a frown.

'Can't I stay a bit longer? There's loads more to do.'

Rick looked at Steph.

'I've promised my father I'll take him to pick up his car later. It's in for a service.'

'Why not leave her here? She seems happy and I'm glad of the help. She seems to know what she's doing.'

He grinned at her.

'Chip off the old block.' He looked back lovingly at Bryony. 'OK, you win. Be good.' He turned to Steph. 'I'll come back for her later. It's good to see her happy.'

He kissed Steph on the cheek, making sure Bryony was looking at her logs rather than at them as he did so.

Steph was trying to reach an awkward branch above the shed roof when the ladder swayed and she felt herself falling. Her hand hit the ground first. Through her daze she was aware of

245

Bryony looming over her, fear in her face. She tried to get up but couldn't put any weight on the arm.

'Shall I get someone?' Bryony was saying.

'Just let me sit here for a while. I'm OK. Just shocked.'

With Bryony's help she managed to get up out of the brambles, over to the garden table. Her arm was very painful.

'I'll phone Dad,' Bryony said. 'He'll know what to do.'

'No, Bryony, I'm sure it's all right. Would you make me a cup of tea? That would help.'

Bryony did as she asked and came back with a mug of tea. It did restore her somewhat and she tried to reassure Bryony that all she needed was to sit for a while.

'Do you want me to get Elsie?' she persisted.

'Bryony, don't fuss! Finish stacking the logs and I'll watch you.'

Reluctantly Bryony left her and continued with her work, but she kept glancing over from time to time.

Half an hour later Rick was there, looking worried.

'I wasn't expecting you till later,' Steph said through her pain.

'I came as soon as Bryony phoned.'

Steph looked at Bryony who was now standing beside them looking sheepish.

'I phoned him when I went in to make your tea. I was worried. You're not cross with me, are you?'

Steph smiled at her and Rick said, 'You did the right thing, sweetheart.'

He examined her arm very gently and then said to Bryony, 'Come on, we're going to the hospital.'

Steph began to protest but he would have none of it.

'You are going to get that arm X-rayed. It could be broken.'

They were at the hospital for what seemed like hours before anyone looked at it, and then only to find it was a bad sprain.

Feeling down, she was silent all the way home, nursing her bandaged wrist.

Rick tried to cheer her up without success, and Bryony fell asleep in the back of the car.

When they got back Bryony was adamant.

'I can't leave Steph with a bad arm. She can't even make herself a cup of tea. I have to stay and look after her.'

Steph said she'd be fine but Rick silenced her.

'She's right. Someone has to look after you.'

'I'm grateful for your concern, but her mother will want her back. She wasn't keen on leaving her this morning.'

Bryony went quiet.

'I'll OK it with her mum,' Rick said. 'If there's a problem I'll come back. But I think she'll be happy to leave her here. She's up to her eyes in sorting out the house.'

She felt too weak to argue. The pain killers were wearing off and all she wanted to do was rest her arm.

When Rick left, Bryony settled in front of the television and Steph dozed in the chair until she was woken by Bryony very gently tapping her good arm. She saw on her watch it was eight o'clock.

'I'm starving,' Bryony said. 'When can we eat?'

'I'm not sure I have much in,' Steph said, feeling guilty that she had agreed to Bryony staying without thinking about how she was going to feed her. 'I think there's some ham in the cupboard and we could pick some tomatoes.' She sighed. 'Not much of a dinner, is it?'

Bryony was standing in front of her, looking excited.

'We could get fish and chips. The van comes today.'

'Is it still Briscoe's? I remember them from when I lived here. Let's go for it!'

It was the best meal Steph had eaten in a long time. They sat in front of the television and ate it out of the paper. Then they both went to bed. Bryony was so tired she could hardly climb the stairs.

Next morning Bryony slept in and

Steph made the most of the peace to phone the office and tell them she wouldn't be able to drive back until her arm was less painful.

'I can work from here. There's a lot of routine stuff I have to catch up on.'

Geoff wasn't pleased but had to accept it.

'But when will you be ready to move to Edinburgh? We can't afford to hang around.'

'Geoff, I'm in a lot of pain and I can't drive. I have to clear my flat out and do a hundred other things. I don't even have anywhere to live up there yet. I need time.'

He sighed and rang off.

When Bryony finally got up she finished off all the rolls and honey Elsie had made for Steph.'

'I need to go home. Mum will want me to collect the eggs. I'll come back later and do your garden if you like. It's a nice garden.'

'That would be great. But only if your mum lets you. I expect there's a lot to do with all those greenhouses. She probably needs your help more than I do.'

'She'll let me,' she said and disappeared out the door.

It was mid-afternoon when she came back, dressed in clean jeans and T-shirt and with some eggs.

'Mum sent them. She said they were to thank you for looking after me.'

Steph took the basket and looked at the eggs covered in dirt, not at all like the ones she got at the shop. She was deeply touched.

'Thank her for me, will you? That was very kind.'

Rick appeared while they were wiping the eggs ready to put in the fridge.

'Bel sent these for you. Said you probably wouldn't be able to carry much till your arm is better.' He put two carrier bags on the kitchen table.

'Golly, I'll have more food than I know what to do with soon.' Again she had a warm glow at the kindness and generosity of everyone.

'Well, we can't have you starving, can we?' He seemed much happier and more relaxed than she had seen him and she made him a coffee and poured some lemonade for Bryony to take into the garden.

'Dad, can I paint the shed?' Bryony was wandering round the garden again while Steph and Rick were sitting outside drinking their coffee, both watching her.

'I don't know. It isn't my shed,' he said.

Bryony came skipping over to them.

'Steph, can I?'

Steph shrugged.

'What colour?'

Bryony gave her a strange look.

'I don't mean a colour. I mean brown. It'll rot if you don't paint it. Some bits are going soggy already.'

'She means preservative,' Rick explained.

'Well, yes, if you want to. We can't have soggy bits, can we? But I don't have any preservative, as far as I know.'

Rick was laughing.

'I'll bring some round if you want. It'll keep her busy.'

When Rick left, Steph tried to do some work on her laptop out in the sun, but her arm still hurt quite a bit. So she abandoned it and sat watching Bryony expertly applying the preservative to the shed and thought how like Rick she was. It was such a peaceful scene with her lovely tubs of flowers and the birds singing.

When the door bell rang she walked through and looked out of the front window. She could see a car parked on the lane and her heart sank. It was Greg.

He stood on the doorstep, looking full of himself as usual, no sign of remorse.

'What are you doing here?' she asked.

'I must say that's a fine welcome for someone who's driven for hours to come and look after you.'

'I don't need looking after,' she snapped.

'So, do I have to turn round and

drive all the way back without even a cup of tea?'

She stood aside so that he could come in. He walked through the cottage and looked out into the garden.

'Not bad. I see you have help.'

'That's Bryony. She's a neighbour's daughter and she's painting my shed.'

She was flustered, not knowing what to do with him. She couldn't turn him away after such a long journey. Maybe she should be grateful he had cared enough to come. Maybe she was being ungrateful, but she didn't want him here.

'Steph, can't we talk? Surely we can remain friends.'

'No. Not after what you did. I could never trust you again after that. And don't try to deny it.'

'I'm not going to deny it. Steph. I'm here to try to explain it.'

'What possible explanation could you have for vandalising my flat?' She was glaring at him.

'The fact that I love you. I wanted to

keep you near me.'

'That's not love. That's manipulation. You thought that by frightening me into thinking I was in danger that you could creep into my life. It's despicable.'

'I know that now. I'm sorry I did it. It was a stupid thing to do. But I was careful not to damage anything. It all went back in place again. I wouldn't have taken anything. I wanted to stop you spending so much time at the cottage. You seemed to be obsessed with it. I was afraid you were going to move there and leave me.'

He looked so dejected she couldn't help feeling a little sorry for him. They had been good friends once and it probably was true that he hadn't meant her any harm. So she made him a cup of tea and they went into the garden and sat at the table.

'I'll have my tea then and find a hotel in Southport. I'm sorry. I thought I was being a friend in need; that I could look after you. I wanted to show you how sorry I am for what I did. I see now that I'm not wanted here.'

'I'm sorry, Greg, it won't work any more.'

'It's OK, Steph. Only I wasn't going to give in without a fight. I care too much.'

She gave a resigned smile.

'I'm sorry you had a wasted journey.'

She couldn't find it in her heart to turn him away without even that. Bryony came up from the garden and stared at him. Steph explained that he was an old friend visiting her and she accepted it.

Greg had just got up to take his leave when Rick came ambling round the side of the cottage. He took in the situation and stopped dead.

Steph introduced the two men and Greg held out his hand. Rick ignored it and Greg let it fall to his side again. Both men looked uneasy. Bryony dragged Rick out to show him her handy work. After taking a look at the shed, he turned to Bryony.

'Right, young lady, I'm taking you home.'

'Why?' Bryony said. 'I haven't finished it yet.'

'You can do it another day. Your mother wants you home now.'

'What for? I did all my chores this morning. She said I could come here for the rest of the day if Steph didn't mind. I'm supposed to be looking after her. You said I could.'

'She doesn't need you to look after her now,' he said. 'We're going home.'

Bryony looked at Steph then shrugged. Rick stood silently, waiting for her. Greg didn't quite know what was going on so sat down again. Bryony went into a sulk but did what she was told and followed Rick out of the garden.

'What was all that about, then?' Greg asked.

Steph shook her head.

'Nothing, her dad's just taking her home, that's all.'

'Seems like a lot more than that to me,' he said.

Steph was too upset to care what Greg thought. She just wanted him out of her garden and out of her life.

He seemed to accept that his visit had been a mistake and quickly departed.

She couldn't drive home. She couldn't do anything useful in the cottage. Even working on her laptop was painful. She was thoroughly fed up.

Well, she wasn't going to let it get her down. She was going to eat some of this food Bel had sent then, then she'd phone Rick and try to explain. She'd tell him that Greg had gone and ask if Bryony could come back tomorrow.

But he wasn't answering his mobile and when she phoned Austin he told her Rick hadn't come home that evening and hadn't phoned to say why.

She told him she'd seen him that afternoon and tried to reassure him that all was well, but she felt uneasy and knew Austin was worried, too.

Almost immediately after she hung up, Sally rang her.

'Rick's just left. He's in a bit of a

state. He's left his car in the car park and he's gone down Bankside Lane towards the marsh. He often goes there when he's upset; says he can think down there. I'm worried about him. He's not his usual self. I thought I'd better let you know.'

Black Clouds Gather

Steph was out of the cottage in no time and on her way to where she knew he'd be. Black clouds were forming and she knew they were in for a summer storm. She hadn't stopped to put a coat on and was already shivering in her sleeveless top and sandals, yet she pressed on, down the lane and over the bank on to the marsh and she saw him.

He was sitting against the grassy bank that acted as a sea wall and staring out to sea, his body hunched against the wind. Slowly she made her way across the turf and over the channels of water until she was beside him. He knew she was there but he didn't turn.

'Greg's gone. He had no business coming here.'

He didn't react to her words.

'Rick, talk to me. This is silly. It's a misunderstanding.'

Then he did turn towards her. His eyes were blazing.

'You deceived me, Steph. You accused me of not putting you in the picture about my ex-wife and daughter. You made me feel guilty and led me to believe you had no attachments. Then you spring this on me.'

'You've got the wrong idea.'

'Have I? That man travels half the length of the country when he hears you've hurt your arm, and you tell me he means nothing to you. Steph, I'm not a fool.'

'Neither am I.' Her tone was measured. 'I have had to learn from everyone else that you've been married, have a child, and then that you were leaving for Cornwall.'

'Why did it matter? I have a history — we all do. Eventually I would have told you about Bryony, and the rest. I can't help it if the village grapevine is more efficient at relating my life story than I am.'

She was silent.

'When did you intend telling me that you had a boyfriend? He definitely didn't seem like an ex to me.'

'He was a friend — that's all he's ever been. And he isn't even that now.'

They stared at each other. There was a clap of thunder and lightning lit the sky. The rain came in a great torrent and Rick grabbed her hand and pulled her with him up the marsh, carefully leading her between the gullies. Her feet squelched in the wet turf and she clung on to him for fear of falling. There was a wooden structure further up the marsh nestled beneath the bank, a hide for bird watchers, and he pulled her inside and held her close to him. Wind tore at the timbers until she feared the whole structure was about to take off. But she felt safe in his arms and they remained like that until the storm eased. Then he let her go.

'It's passed over,' he said.

Steph went through the door and into the rain, which was gentle now, and the sky had lightened. She turned to him.

'Will you come back with me?'

'No, I'll stay here a while.' The anger had gone from his voice.

She climbed the bank which led back to the lane. Her heart felt like it would break. Not even after Simon had left had she felt so bereft.

When she got home she phoned Austin and told him what had happened.

'He always went there when he was upset, even when he was a boy. He'll come home soon. Don't worry.'

But she worried all night. All she could think of was Rick down there, thinking she had betrayed him.

She was on her way to get milk from Bel next morning when a car passed her then turned in a farm gate a few yards down the lane and came back towards her. She looked to see who it was and saw it was Austin. Her heart lifted. He was smiling and jumped out as soon as he'd drawn alongside her.

'My dear, where are you off to? Can I give you a lift?'

'Austin, what are you doing here?'

'I came to see you. You sounded like a damsel in distress, so here is your knight in shining armour.'

She hugged him and they both got in the car.

'Right, if you have no urgent business, I suggest lunch at my club. It's very quiet on Thursdays so we can chat and not be disturbed and they do a very acceptable menu. What do you say to that?'

'I'd say you're definitely my knight in shining armour.'

His club was on one of the many golf courses for which the area was famous. It overlooked the green and was airy and pleasant and soon they were sitting by a large window in a quiet corner and studying a menu.

'I suggest the trout. It really is very good,' Austin said and Steph was happy to go along with that. She felt herself relax.

'Now tell me what is going on,' Austin said. 'My son is acting very strangely. One minute you have Bryony staying with you and Rick is happy at last. Then he comes home last night tense and moody after he'd spent most of the evening stalking the marsh.'

She looked into his kind face.

'Where do I begin?'

'Rick is very fond of you. And I suspect you feel the same way about him. Is that so?'

She wasn't going to deny it. Something about Austin drew the truth from her.

'Yes, it's true. But there are so many problems. I can't see any way through them.'

'So what are these insurmountable problems?'

It felt good to talk and soon everything that was troubling Steph came pouring out, finishing with Rick believing that she and Greg were an item, and his reaction when he had seen them together.

'That just shows how much he cares about you. If he didn't care, it wouldn't matter.'

She was very quiet. Austin had a point. Why hadn't she realised that.

'Austin, you are such a tonic for me. Thank you.'

'You have nothing to thank me for, my dear. I want to see my son happy, and you, of course.'

Austin asked for the bill and Steph put her jacket on. When Austin had dropped her off she phoned Geoff to say she was ready for Edinburgh as soon as she could drive. She began to pack up the few things she wanted to keep.

Then she went down to the pub for the evening to try to put everything out of her mind. After a couple of glasses of wine and a chat with Sally, she began to unwind and spent a pleasant few hours with the locals who came in.

Samantha phoned her next morning.

'Steph, Geoff wants you in his office on Monday morning. He wants to discuss your move to Edinburgh.'

'I've told him I can't drive with this arm.'

'You could get a train.'

Steph felt her pulse rise dramatically and could feel a cold sweat breaking out.

'I don't know. I've got the house clearance people coming today, and I have things still to arrange. I need to stay where I am for the time being. Will you tell him that?'

Ten minutes later Geoff was on the phone to her.

'What's this I hear? Yesterday you seemed to have everything under control. What's changed?'

'I'm not ready yet. Can't I just have a bit more time?'

'You can't stand still in this game, Steph. I'm not where I am now through standing still.' He ranted on a bit longer then told her to think it through. 'I'm beginning to wonder if you are really committed to this job.'

After she'd put down the phone she sat for some time staring out at the garden, then picked it up again and called his number.

'Geoff, I've thought about it.'

'Good girl. I knew common sense would prevail in the end. When can you start?'

'I'm not going to start. I rang to say I want to hand in my resignation.'

There was silence at the end of the phone. Then she heard him clearing his throat. His voice was measured now.

'Steph, take more time if you must. There's no pressure. Just don't act rashly.'

'I'm not acting rashly. I mean it, Geoff. I am handing in my notice. That's final.'

In the end he told her he would phone her in a couple of days. She told him she wouldn't change her mind. He wasn't convinced and rang off.

She was shaking now. What had she done? She had worked for years hoping for this opportunity and now she had turned it down. Not only turned the promotion down, but resigned from the company.

The cottage was empty in a very short time and she was reduced to sitting on the floor. She just couldn't get her head round it all. She had been offered a job she had coveted for years and she'd turned it down. She had given up everything she valued; her job, her ambition, her cottage. And for what?

It was late afternoon and she had just finished cleaning the floors one-handed when Rick turned up. He was horrified to see how quickly things had changed.

'Where's your friend?'

She leaned the mop against the wall and faced him.

'I tried to tell you. He wasn't invited and he didn't stay,' she told him. 'And that is all he was. A friend.'

Rick looked into her eyes and she felt a pull stronger than any she had ever felt and a terrible emptiness engulfed her. She followed him into the front room where he stood surveying the emptiness. He turned to her, his face stricken.

'Why have you done this?' he asked.

'I had to,' she said. 'There's nothing for me here.'

'You have everything here; your cottage, friends, memories.' He paused and his eyes held hers. She barely heard his next words. 'And you have me.'

When his words penetrated her brain it was as if something inside her sprang to life.

He stood very still, his expression unfathomable.

'Steph, don't go.'

No words would come, just a great welling of love.

'Steph, I love you. You love me.'

When the words came it seemed someone else was uttering them, as if a well-rehearsed speech.

'No,' she heard herself saying. 'I have to go.'

'Why? You love me. don't you?'

'I don't know. We have different lives in different places. You've found what you've always wanted.' She felt his arms encircle her, his cheek next to hers.

'Yes,' he said. 'I've found what I've always wanted.'

She wasn't listening.

'I'm going home. The cottage is sold.'

'But what about Edinburgh?' His breath was warm on her cheek, his voice soft.

'I'm not going to Edinburgh.'

Then he turned her to face him but still she didn't look up. He tilted her chin and his look was tender.

'Why not, Steph?'

Her voice was flat.

He let her go, his expression changing, his eyes taking on a harder look.

'Yes, I understand. You won't leave Greg.' He said it so softly she could barely hear him and before she could answer he was backing away from her. As he walked out the door she felt she had never endured such pain.

She heard all the gossip when she went to see Elsie a couple of hours later to say goodbye. Austin had booked her into a hotel and was coming to collect her.

'You won't believe the upheaval over at Rick's place.'

'Why, what's happening?' Steph asked.

271

'Rick's off to his new job on some country estate. What a to-do.'

Where Elsie had got this from Steph couldn't imagine, but she knew how the village grapevine worked. There wasn't much Elsie didn't pick up one way or another.

Steph walked back to the cottage. Rick had gone. He'd told her he loved her and she'd pushed him away. She would never see him again. Finally it was over.

As she put the key in the cottage door a big black cloud descended on her, nearly drowning her in gloom. She couldn't do it. She gripped the door frame. She just couldn't do it. Something had changed her. It was this cottage, this village. And Rick. No matter what happened, she knew for certain she couldn't go back.

It was then that Austin's words came back to her.

'Do you love each other enough?' He had known how she felt, had recognised the signs, had experienced them himself and knew the pain of loss.

Could she bear to live for the rest of her life with such pain, knowing the man she loved was out there and wanted her as much as she wanted him?

She didn't even shut the door, but ran back to the village and on to Boland's. What she would do when she got there she didn't know. She just had to get there and tell him she loved him and that she couldn't live without him.

He wasn't there. Gary looked at her in alarm when he saw the state she was in.

'What's up? You look right bothered. Rick's gone. It's been a right carry on here today, I can tell you. Fiona's been ranting on about him leaving. He wouldn't listen, just kept throwing things in bags and loading his car and giving out orders. I've never seen him in such a state.'

She had to see Rick. She'd left it too long and whatever it took now she had to let him know how she felt. She turned and fled. She had to drive to

Southport. He wouldn't go without seeing his father. She could do it. Her car was an automatic. She only needed one good arm.

Rick was sitting outside the cottage waiting for her. He walked round the side of the cottage and into the garden. There was something about him that stopped her from speaking. Standing behind him by the pond she bit her lip to try to gain control again but couldn't stop shaking.

'Rick, what's wrong?'

He turned to look at her, his face tense.

'I want to know why you are going back to London. Is it the job, Steph, or is it Greg? I want the truth.'

She couldn't answer; her voice wouldn't come.

He persisted, his face more determined than she'd ever seen it.

'Why not Edinburgh? It was what you wanted. It can only be about Greg. Why else would you give up an opportunity like that?'

She looked at his expression, so grave she found it almost impossible to control her voice.

'It has nothing to do with Greg. I just can't face a new place alone.'

Something changed in his expression.

'Steph, you wouldn't be alone.'

'I would be.' She sobbed.

He took hold of her firmly by the shoulders.

'Steph, listen to me. You won't be alone in Edinburgh.'

She pulled away and looked out over the garden.

'I don't know what I want.' She took a deep breath then the words came out. 'I love you and I want us to be together, but I don't know how. You're off to Cornwall.'

'I'm not going anywhere without you, my darling.'

She was startled out of her misery.

'You can't give up the job you've always wanted.'

'Yes, I can. I will stay here with you if that will make you happy, if you really don't want to move to Edinburgh.'

'But this is your big opportunity.'

'What about your big opportunity?'

She was silent. It was impossible to control her voice enough to answer.

His face had lost its anger as he looked into her eyes.

'We both had a dream, Steph. Until you came along I never thought I could do it. You encouraged me to do it.'

'Then you must,' she said with some effort.

'And so must you, Steph.'

She was about to protest again but he silenced her.

'I am not giving anything up. I'm simply changing direction. I have the offer of a job on an estate near Andrew. I made up my mind to do everything possible for us to have a future together.'

He took her in his arms and she dissolved in the love and security they held. Here was a man she could trust for ever.

They clung together for a very long time, then she pushed at his chest so she could look at him again.

Taking his chance, Rick asked what he had wanted to for a long time.

'Will you marry me?'

Then she was in his arms and they were hugging and kissing all over again. Then he held her away from him and looked deep into her eyes. She smiled up at him, her eyes bright with tears.

Rick took her hand and pulled her over to the pond. He bent and eased the moss aside from the writing on the stone. She bent beside him and they gazed at it together, and she traced a finger round the lettering.

'Rose wasn't able to follow her dream, but she made sure I followed mine. That's why she left me the cottage.'

They heard a car pull up on the gravel.

'I think that is your chauffeur come to take madam to her hotel,' Rick joked.

She couldn't stop laughing.

'And would sir like to join me for dinner?'

'I think that could be arranged.'

Steph was unpacking her suitcase when her mobile rang. It was Greta.

'Steph, I have some news.' She didn't give Steph a chance to speak. 'Greg has fallen in love. He brought this girl to the club last night. She's just right for him, very pretty and hangs on his every word.' She paused. 'He's worried about how you'll react. You don't mind, do you?'

Steph was grinning into the phone.

'I'm glad he's found someone to make him happy.' She told her about the latest developments with Rick.

'Will Rick mind me coming to visit you in Scotland?'

Steph smiled into the phone.

'Greta, you will always be welcome. Anyway, I have to go. My wonderful man will be here soon to take me to tea.'

'Oh, you lucky girl. Have a wonderful time.'

When Rick arrived, he asked her if

she minded if he took her out to dinner instead of eating in the hotel.

'I don't mind at all,' she told him.

They drove out of Southport and she was surprised when they headed for the village, but she could get nothing out of him. He sat staring through the windscreen with a smug look on his face.

They parked in the pub car park and he took her hand and led her inside. The place was packed. Sally was standing behind the bar with a bottle of champagne in her hand. There were tables laid with food and streamers and balloons hanging from every wall.

Elsie and Jim were sitting in one corner. Bryony came running up to them and hugged Rick.

'It was my idea to have a party,' she said proudly. 'Alex and I did the decorations. Do you like them?'

Bel was smiling at her and even Fiona came over and wished them luck.

'I think she's drinking a toast to getting rid of me,' Rick whispered in Steph's ear.

'We couldn't let you go without a send off,' Sally said.

Steph was speechless. She felt so lucky. Silently she sent a big thank-you to Rose.

It was much later when Rick dropped her off at her hotel. He took her up to her room and took her in his arms.

'Are you sure you want to marry me?' he asked.

She held a finger to his mouth as he bent to kiss her.

'I have never been more sure of anything in my life,' she said as they melted into each other's arms.

THE END

We do hope that you have enjoyed reading this large print book.

Did you know that all of our titles are available for purchase?

We publish a wide range of high quality large print books including:
Romances, Mysteries, Classics
General Fiction
Non Fiction and Westerns

Special interest titles available in large print are:
The Little Oxford Dictionary
Music Book, Song Book
Hymn Book, Service Book

Also available from us courtesy of Oxford University Press:
Young Readers' Dictionary
(large print edition)
Young Readers' Thesaurus
(large print edition)

For further information or a free brochure, please contact us at:
Ulverscroft Large Print Books Ltd.,
The Green, Bradgate Road, Anstey,
Leicester, LE7 7FU, England.
Tel: (00 44) 0116 236 4325
Fax: (00 44) 0116 234 0205

Other titles in the
Linford Romance Library:

AN UNEXPECTED ENCOUNTER

Fenella Miller

Miss Victoria Marsh has an unexpected encounter in the church with a handsome, but disagreeable, soldier who is recuperating from a grievous leg injury. Major Toby Highcliff believes himself to be a useless cripple, but meeting Victoria changes everything. Will he be able to keep her safe from the evil that stalks the neighbourhood and convince her he is the ideal man for her?